D1375494

16

A MAP OF THE WORLD

Also by David Hare

SLAG
TEETH 'N' SMILES
KNUCKLE
FANSHEN
PLENTY

Films for television

LICKING HITLER
DREAMS OF LEAVING
SAIGON

A Map of the World

DAVID HARE

BIRKBECK
LIBRARY
COLLEGE

faber and faber

First published in 1982
by Faber and Faber Limited
3 Queen Square London WC1N 3AU
The first edition was for sale in Australia and New Zealand only
This second, revised edition first published 1983
Printed in Great Britain by
Latimer Trend & Company Ltd Plymouth

All rights reserved

© David Hare, 1982, 1983

All rights whatsoever in this play are strictly
reserved and applications for permission to perform
it, etc. must be made in advance, before rehearsals
begin, to Margaret Ramsay Ltd., 14a Goodwin's
Court, St Martin's Lane, London WC2

CONDITIONS OF SALE
This book is sold subject to the condition that it shall not, by way
of trade or otherwise, be lent, re-sold, hired out or otherwise
circulated without the publisher's prior consent in any form of
binding or cover other than that in which it is published and
without a similar condition including this condition being
imposed on the subsequent purchaser

British Library Cataloguing in Publication Data

Hare, David
A map of the world.—2nd rev. ed.
I. Title
822'. 914   PR6058.A/

ISBN 0-571-11996-4

For
DEBORAH EISENBERG
and
WALLACE SHAWN

A map of the world that does not include Utopia is not worth even glancing at, for it leaves out the one country at which Humanity is always landing. And when Humanity lands there, it looks out, and, seeing a better country, sets sail.

OSCAR WILDE
'The Soul of Man Under Socialism'

CHARACTERS

ELAINE LE FANU
STEPHEN ANDREWS
VICTOR MEHTA
PEGGY WHITTON
ANGELIS
MARTINSON
M'BENGUE

WAITERS
CREW
ASSISTANTS
DIPLOMATS
etc.

A Map of the World was presented at the Opera Theatre, Adelaide, and subsequently at the Sydney Opera House in March 1982. The cast was as follows:

ELAINE LE FANU	Sheila Scott Wilkinson
STEPHEN ANDREWS	Robert Grubb
VICTOR MEHTA	Roshan Seth
PEGGY WHITTON	Penny Downie
ANGELIS	Peter Whitford
MARTINSON	Tim Robertson
M'BENGUE	Desiré Vincent
SCRIPT GIRL	Andrea Moore
FILM ASSISTANTS	Hugo Weaving
	Michael O'Neill

Directed by David Hare
Designed by Hayden Griffin *and* Eamon D'Arcy
Lighting by Rory Dempster
Music by Nick Bicat

The play was presented at the Lyttleton Theatre, London, on 20 January 1983. It was directed by David Hare and designed by Hayden Griffin.

ACT ONE

Scene One. *A hotel lounge. Crumbling grandeur. Cane chairs. A great expanse of black-and-white checked floor stretching back into the distance. Porticos. Windows at the back and, to one side, oak doors. But the scene must only be sketched in, not realistically complete.*

STEPHEN *is sitting alone, surrounded by international newspapers, which he is reading. He is in his late twenties, but still boyish: tall, thin, dry. He is wearing seersucker trousers, and his jacket is over the chair. He has a now-emptied glass of beer and a bottle beside him. He is English.*

ELAINE *comes through the oak doors, sheets of Gestetnered material in her hand. She is about thirty-five, disarmingly smart and well dressed. Her elegance seems not at all ruffled by the heat. She is a black American.*

ELAINE: The heat.

STEPHEN: I know.

(ELAINE *goes to the back to look in vain for a waiter.*)
Are they still talking?

ELAINE: Yes.

STEPHEN: Ah.

ELAINE: The Senegalese delegate is just about to start.

(*She wanders back down, nodding at one of his magazines.*)
Is that *Newsweek*?

STEPHEN: Yes. There's nothing about us.

(*He has picked it up and now reads from it.*)
'Tracy Underling of Dayton, Ohio, has the rest of her downtown, largely Catholic Santa Maria College class in thrall with the size of her exceptional IQ, which local psycho-expert Lorne Schlitz claims tops genius level at 175. Says the bearded Schlitz: "Proof of her abundant intelligence

11

is that she has already begun writing her third novel at the age of five." Subject of the novel will be the life of Mary Tyler Moore . . .'

(ELAINE *smiles and walks away*.)

ELAINE: America!

STEPHEN: I mean, who actually writes this stuff?

ELAINE: Is it any worse than ours?

(STEPHEN *smiles slightly*.)

That M'Bengue is appalling.

STEPHEN: Who?

ELAINE: The Senegalese. He's raising his third point of order.

STEPHEN: It's a compulsion . . .

ELAINE: Yes.

STEPHEN: . . . I'm afraid.

(ELAINE, *at the back, has a sudden burst of impatience*.)

ELAINE: *Why* are there no waiters?

STEPHEN: Because the bar is nowhere near the lounge. In India no bar is anywhere near any lounge in order that five people may be employed to go backwards and forwards between where the drinkers are and where the drink is. Thus the creation of four unnecessary jobs. Thus the creation of what is called a high-labour economy. Thus low wages. Thus the perpetuation of poverty. Thus going screaming out of your head at the damn bloody obstinacy of the people.

(*He shouts*.) Waiter!

ELAINE: Thus dying of thirst.

STEPHEN: Well, yes. Not the most tactful remark in the circumstances.

(*He looks across at* ELAINE *who has sat down and is flicking through a magazine. But she seems unconcerned*.)

I had a friend who rang me and said, 'Is your hotel in a bad area?' I said, 'Well, quite bad.' She said, 'Does it have corpses?' I said, 'Well, no.' She said, 'Well, mine actually has corpses.' And she was right. When I went to see her, there are people who sleep on the pavement . . . who have failed to wake . . . who are just lying there with rats running over them . . .

ELAINE: Bombay's quite prosperous.

STEPHEN: I know. I know. It's a thriving, commercial city of two
million people. Only there happen to be seven million
people living there, which leaves the extra five million
looking pretty stupid every night.

ELAINE: All right.

STEPHEN: Well.

ELAINE: If that's what you feel, go and say it in there.

(*He looks across at her. She has gone back to reading.*)

STEPHEN: I would if I could be heard among the clamour of
voices. Is there not something ludicrous in holding an
international conference on poverty in these spectacular
surroundings, when all we would actually have to do is to
take one step into the street to see exactly what the
problems of poverty are?

ELAINE: Most of the delegates have.

STEPHEN: Then why is their interest entirely in striking attitudes
and making procedural points?

ELAINE: Because that's politics.

STEPHEN: You accept that?

ELAINE: Of course.

STEPHEN: (*His voice rising*) When even now out in the streets . . .

ELAINE: It's the dirt that disgusts you, that's all.

STEPHEN: What?

(ELAINE *has put her magazine aside, suddenly deciding to take
him on.*)

ELAINE: I've watched you the last couple of days . . .

STEPHEN: I see.

ELAINE: . . . since we met. You're like everyone. You can't
understand why the peasants should choose to leave the
countryside, where they can die a nice clean death from
starvation, to come and grub around in the filthy gutter,
where they do, however, have some small chance of life.

STEPHEN: That's not quite true.

ELAINE: It shocks you that people prefer to live in cardboard,
they prefer to live in excrement, in filth, than go back and
die on the land. But they do. And as you want drama, and
as this is your third day in India . . .

STEPHEN: Fourth.

ELAINE: . . . you're determined to find this bad. Because you
come from the West and are absolutely set on having an
experience, so you find it necessary to dramatize. You come
absolutely determined in advance to find India shocking, and
so you can't see that underneath it all there is a great deal
about the life here which isn't too bad.
(*She turns back. Quietly:*)
At least, if you'd covered Vietnam, that's how you'd feel.
(STEPHEN *looks at her a moment.*)

STEPHEN: No, well, of course, I'm not an old hand.

ELAINE: No.

STEPHEN: I'm just a journalist from England.

ELAINE: Quite.

STEPHEN: On a literary left-wing magazine, therefore by
definition—what is it?—*parti pris*.

ELAINE: That's right.

STEPHEN: But nevertheless, perhaps I . . .

ELAINE: What?

STEPHEN: . . . can see it with an eye which . . .

ELAINE: If you . . .

STEPHEN: What?
(ELAINE *rides right over him with sudden and surprising
forcefulness.*)

ELAINE: It's just that I can't stand to see people making value
judgements about other people's ways of life. The
hippopotamus, if I may say so, may be perfectly happy in
the mud.

STEPHEN: And the Indian, I suppose you think, is perfectly
happy in his excrement.

ELAINE: No, I didn't say that.

STEPHEN: Well!

ELAINE: But it's arrogant to look at the world . . .

STEPHEN: I'm not.

ELAINE: . . . through one . . .

STEPHEN: All right.

ELAINE: . . . particular perspective which is always to say, 'This
is like the West. This is not like the West.' What
arrogance!

14

STEPHEN: No, well, I can't see that . . .

ELAINE: If I may . . . *say* . . .

(And suddenly the steam goes.)

STEPHEN: Sorry.

ELAINE: All right.

STEPHEN: Well . . .

(A pause.)

ELAINE: God, this conference.

STEPHEN: I know.

(There is another pause, the two of them suspended. Then a cry from STEPHEN:)

Waiter!

(He turns back to ELAINE.)

It makes you so ill-tempered. You think you'll go for a stroll. 'I wouldn't leave the hotel if I were you, sir,' they say. 'The monsoon is coming.' With a great grin appearing on their faces as if the thought of it just suited them fine. 'Ah, good, the monsoon.' And you caught in it best of all. I suppose it's the only revenge the poor have, that their land is uninhabitable by anyone but themselves. That we can't drink their water, or eat their food, or walk in their streets without getting mobbed, or endure their weather, or even, in fact, if we are truthful, contemplate their lives . . .

ELAINE: Stephen . . .

(She smiles.)

You exaggerate again.

(At the opposite side to the conference hall VICTOR MEHTA has appeared. He is in his early forties. He is wearing a light brown suit and tie and he has thick black hair. He is an Indian, but his manners are distinctly European.)

MEHTA: This is UNESCO?

STEPHEN: Yes. The conference on poverty.

MEHTA: Ah.

(MEHTA turns at once and summons a white-coated boy from offstage.)

Waiter.

WAITER: Sir?

MEHTA: Can you see my bags are taken to my room?

15

STEPHEN: Ah, you found a waiter.

MEHTA: Certainly. There is no problem, is there?

(*He turns back to the* WAITER.)

And bring me a bottle of white wine. Is there a Pouilly Fuissé?

WAITER: Pouilly Fumé, sir.

MEHTA: Then I will drink champagne.

(*The* WAITER *goes. The three of them stand a moment. A chilly smile from* MEHTA.)

So.

STEPHEN: Please sit down. They are expecting you, I think . . .

MEHTA: Good.

STEPHEN: . . . in the conference. This is Elaine le Fanu from CBS network.

(*They shake hands.*)

ELAINE: Very nice to meet you.

STEPHEN: Stephen Andrews.

MEHTA: And you are a journalist as well?

STEPHEN: Of a kind.

(*They have all sat down.* STEPHEN *smiles, anticipating* MEHTA's *views.*)

You're very hard on journalists in your books.

MEHTA: I?

(*He thinks about this a moment, as if it had never occurred to him.*)

No.

STEPHEN: *The Vermin Class.* It's not a flattering title for a novel on our profession.

MEHTA: I'm sure Miss le Fanu is not vermin.

(*He is looking straight at* ELAINE, *the sustained stare of the philanderer.*)

STEPHEN: No.

ELAINE: Have you come far?

MEHTA: I left Heathrow ten hours ago. I left Shropshire—

ELAINE: Your home?

MEHTA: Yes—even earlier.

STEPHEN: Are you speaking tomorrow?

MEHTA: Yes. A chore. To be frank. The necessary prostitution of

16

the intellect. So much is demanded now of the writer which is not writing, which is not the work. The work alone ought to be sufficient. But my publishers plead with me to make myself seen.

STEPHEN: I think you'll find there's great anticipation. I mean, there's some interest as to what you'll say.

(MEHTA *looks away, indifferent.*)

Particularly the comparison with China. It's impossible here not to compare the two cultures . . .

MEHTA: Yes?

STEPHEN: I mean, the way the one is so organized, the other, India, so . . . Well, this is a theme you have dealt with in your books.

MEHTA: I suppose.

(*He is still for a moment, lizard-like. Just as* STEPHEN *starts again, he interrupts.*)

STEPHEN: If . . .

MEHTA: Of the Chinese leadership the only one I was able to bring myself to admire wholeheartedly was Chou en-Lai.

ELAINE: Ah.

MEHTA: Because he alone among the leaders had the iron self-control not to use his position to publish his own poetry. Chairman Mao, unhappily, not so.

ELAINE: Yes.

(ELAINE *smiles, looks down at the ground, knowingly, having dealt with many such men.*)

Do you not admire Mao?

MEHTA: How can I? Like so many senior statesmen, he decided to ruin his credibility by marrying an actress. How is it possible to believe in a man who does such a thing?

ELAINE: Well . . .

MEHTA: And what an actress! We are told she was born beautiful, but as an act of identification with the masses, she willed herself ugly.

(*He smiles at* ELAINE, *contemptuously.*)

But even if it were true, the method hardly matters. The results of the policy are only too plain to see.

(STEPHEN *is frowning.*)

STEPHEN: But there are elements of China . . .

17

MEHTA: What?

STEPHEN: . . . elements of the Chinese experiment you admire?

MEHTA: I admire nothing in the experiment. I admire China itself.

(*As he speaks,* WAITERS *enter in rough formation carrying, one by one, a bucket, a bottle, a bag of ice, and glasses.*)

Ah, champagne.

(*As he speaks, the glasses are distributed, the bucket set down.*)

All old civilizations are superior to younger ones. That is why I have been happiest in Shropshire. They are less subject to crazes. In younger countries there is no culture. The civilization is shallow. Nothing takes root. Gangs of crazy youths sweep through the streets of Sydney and New York pretending they are homosexual. But do you think they are homosexual really? Of course not. It is the merest fashion. City fashion, that is all. In the old countries, in Paris, in London, when there is a stupid craze, only one person in fifty is infected, but in the young countries there is nothing to hold people back. It is suddenly like the worm factory, everybody fucks everybody, until the next craze, and then everyone will move on and forget and settle down with young women who sell handbags. But meanwhile the damage has been done. The plant has been pulled up at the root, and violently plunged back into the earth, so the slow process of growing must begin again. But a worthwhile civilization takes two thousand years to grow.

(*The* WAITERS *have left.* MEHTA *leans forward to pour himself champagne.*)

STEPHEN: Yes, but . . .

(*He gestures at the bottle.*)

May I? Surely—

(MEHTA *has taken one sip and puts his glass aside, where he leaves it, untouched.*)

MEHTA: It is not good.

STEPHEN: Surely there's a problem, if what you say is true?

(STEPHEN *has got up to pour out a glass for himself and* ELAINE.)

Do you say to those young countries, to so many countries

18

represented in that room, countries with no traditions, no institutions, no civilization as we know it, no old ways of ordering themselves—what do you say? 'Sorry, things will take time . . . it may be bloody in your country at first, but this is an inevitable phase in a *young* civilization. You must endure dictatorship and bloodshed and barbarity . . .

ELAINE: Mr Mehta wasn't saying that.

STEPHEN: . . . because you are young. There is nothing we can do for you.'

ELAINE: This is . . .

STEPHEN: No, surely not! They must be helped!

MEHTA: Nobody can help.

STEPHEN: What do you mean?

MEHTA: Except by example. By what one is. One is civilized. One is cultured. One is rational. That is how you help other people to live.

(*He smiles at* ELAINE, *as if only she will understand.* STEPHEN *is staring in disbelief.*)

STEPHEN: You mean you are saying . . . even as someone reaches up to you to be fed . . .

ELAINE: That isn't . . .

MEHTA: If I may . . .

STEPHEN: 'Oh, no I can't fill your bowl . . .

ELAINE: Stephen . . .

STEPHEN: . . . but I would—please—do—like you to admire my civilization, the cut of my suit!'

(MEHTA *is smiling at* ELAINE, *to say he can deal with this.*)

MEHTA: All right, well, really, you proceed by parody.

STEPHEN: No.

ELAINE: Stephen's . . .

STEPHEN: No. What you are *saying* . . .

ELAINE: (*With sudden violence*) Mr *Mehta* has written about this.

(*There is a pause.* STEPHEN *walks a long way upstage. Pauses. Turns. Walks back down. Picks the bottle out and pours himself another glass. Sits down again. Then* MEHTA *speaks very calmly.*)

MEHTA: It is true that it is hard . . . it is hard to help the poor. Young men like you, who have left the universities, find this sort of talk easy, just as any woman may make a group of men feel guilty with feminist ideas—how easy it is, at dinner tables, to make all the men feel bad, how we do not do our share, how we do not care for their cunts, how their orgasms are not of the right kind, how this, how that, this piece of neglect, this wrong thinking or that—so it is with you, you young men of Europe. You make us all uncomfortable by saying 'The poor! The poor!' But the poor are a convenience only, a prop you use to express your own discontent. Which is with yourself.

(*There is a pause.*)

(*Darkly*) I have known many men like you.

(ELAINE *is slightly shocked by* MEHTA's *cruelty. But suddenly he seems to relax again.*)

The subject was not the poor. I was not speaking of them. The subject was Australia, and why Barry is suddenly in the in the bed of Bruce. Do you have views on that?

STEPHEN: No.

MEHTA: Well, no. Because there is no political explanation, so it bores you.

STEPHEN: Did I say?

MEHTA: I know you. I know it from your look.

(*He turns away, shaking his head.*)

Politics. It is the disease. Narrow politics. The old Jew-bastard Marx . . .

STEPHEN: Well . . .

MEHTA: The inflammation of the intellect among the young, the distortion. Every idea crammed through this tiny ideology, everything crammed through the eye of Marxism. Tssh! What nonsense it all is.

(*He turns back to* STEPHEN.)

(*Definitively*) Socialism, a luxury of the wealthy. To the poor, a suicidal creed.

(*Then he gets up, smiling pleasantly, as if the day's work were done.*)

Well, I am tired of arguing . . .

STEPHEN: Actually, you haven't argued at all.

MEHTA: What do you mean?

ELAINE: Stephen.

STEPHEN: I don't call what he does arguing at all. You've attributed to me various views which you say I hold—on what evidence I have no idea. Marx you mention. I didn't mention him, or universities, or what I'm supposed to think about the poor. I've said nothing. It was you who dragged it in, just as you dragged in all that peculiar and rather distasteful talk about women's orgasms—something, I must say, I rather gather from your books you have the utmost difficulty in coming to terms with . . .

MEHTA: (*Inflamed*) Ah, now I see!

STEPHEN: Yes!

MEHTA: Underneath all the talk . . .

STEPHEN: Yes!

MEHTA: . . . all the apparent concern for the poor, now we have the true thing, what we really want to say, what he really has to say: he has read my books! And of course he must hurt me.

(STEPHEN *looks down. He answers, still stubborn but also feeble.*)

STEPHEN: I certainly do think they are not very pro-women.

(MEHTA *glowers at him.*)

MEHTA: Ah, well, of course, the ultimate progressive offence among the young men from the universities. In the old days—what was it?—that one must be pro-life; now we must be pro-women . . .

STEPHEN: No.

MEHTA: Well, ask yourself if your heroes are very pro-women, your Lenin, your Castro . . .

STEPHEN: He is not *my* Castro.

MEHTA: This ludicrous, long-winded bore who speaks for eight hours on end, who won his battles by speaking whole villages to death—they reeled over, bored in the face of his speeches—this man (we do not say this, it is long forgotten) who was once an extra in an Esther Williams movie. Splash! It is the right noise for him. Splash and yawn!

STEPHEN: There, you're doing it again. I haven't mentioned Castro.

MEHTA: At a conference on poverty, 'Castro! Castro!' It is the chorus of sheep.

STEPHEN: Why do you come? Why do you come here if it's such torture to you?

MEHTA: Yes. And why are you here?

(*There is a sudden pause, after the shouting. Sure of his point,* MEHTA *now formally turns to* ELAINE.)

Miss le Fanu, tonight I am to dine with the Professor of Classical Studies at New Delhi University. It is already pre-arranged. He is coming specially, he is flying, as he is keen to hear my views on his new translation of Herodotus.

(STEPHEN *speaks quietly as he helps himself, a little drunkenly, to more champagne.*)

STEPHEN: Oh, shit!

MEHTA: (*Ignoring this*) If our conversation would not be tedious to you, I would be delighted if you would join us for dinner, and afterwards perhaps . . .

STEPHEN: He could fuck your arse ragged in an upstairs room.

(*An explosion from the others.*)

MEHTA: Mr Andrews!

ELAINE: I must say, Stephen . . .

MEHTA: I cannot see how that remark is justified.

(STEPHEN *smiles, hovering, drunk, magnificent.*)

STEPHEN: How the right wing always appropriate good manners. Yes? They always have that. Form and decorum. A permanent excuse for not addressing themselves to what people actually say, because they can always turn their heads away if a sentence is not correctly formulated.

MEHTA: Now it is you who are exaggerating.

STEPHEN: You're like all those people who think that if you say 'Excuse me' at one end of a sentence and 'Thank you' at the other, you are entitled to be as rude as you like in between. English manners!

MEHTA: Whatever one may think of them, it seems it is only the foreigner who bothers with them any more.

STEPHEN: Yes. How appropriate! That you, an Indian by birth, should be left desperately mimicking the manners of a

22

country that died—died in its heart—over twenty, thirty, forty years ago.

(*He gestures to the ceiling of the room.*)

This sad, pathetic imitation, this room, this conference, these servants—that all this goes on, like a ghost ship without passengers. Form without content. Style without meaning. The India of the rich! How I despise it!

MEHTA: Yes.

(MEHTA *looks at him, watching, not rising to the bait.*)

ELAINE: You're smiling.

MEHTA: Yes. It makes me smile suddenly to see the young man . . .

STEPHEN: Stephen.

MEHTA: . . . to see Stephen gesturing. To hear him argue. His voice goes up to the big ceiling. I am at home again. This is India and we are arguing. In Hindi there is no word for 'eavesdropper'. It is not needed. Everyone speaks too loud. When I think of my home, it is of men in rooms arguing. And in the streets, the dying. This is India. Without the will to act.

(*His sudden characteristic darkness has come over him. Then he turns to* ELAINE.)

Miss le Fanu, you are welcome to dine with us.

ELAINE: Thank you.

MEHTA: I have asked your Peggy Whitton.

ELAINE: Our who?

MEHTA: The Peggy Whitton whom I met just now.

ELAINE: Do we know her?

STEPHEN: Dark. Attractive.

MEHTA: She is attractive, yes.

STEPHEN: But she said . . .

MEHTA: What?

STEPHEN: . . . that she would dine with me.

(MEHTA *looks at him.*)

MEHTA: Well, it is a penalty of your rudeness to lose her.

(*He turns.*)

Miss le Fanu, the invitation is open.

ELAINE: Thank you.

METHA: Drink my wine, please. It is for you.

(*He goes. A silence.* STEPHEN *wanders away. Then quietly*:)

STEPHEN: Drink my wine, please. It is for you.

(ELAINE *smiles to herself.*)

You're not . . .?

ELAINE: Yes. I'll go. He's funny.

STEPHEN: *Why?*

(*His back is turned to her.*)

ELAINE: (*Quietly*) You had your eye on Peggy Whitton, huh?

(STEPHEN, *unseen, is still a moment. Then he turns.*)

STEPHEN: No, of course not. It's his arguments . . .

ELAINE: Ah.

STEPHEN: They're so odious, so offensive . . .

ELAINE: Of course . . .

STEPHEN: As if India were special in some way. As if they
couldn't see there's a belt across the world this thick . . .

(*He holds out a finger and thumb.*)

South America, Africa, Asia—nothing special about being
born into that. It's just where the poor do happen to live,
and most of them get on with the day-to-day business of
being poor . . .

ELAINE: Sure.

STEPHEN: Only here for some reason they can't quite face it, so
they have to say it's holy. They invent this poisonous idea
that it's holy to be poor: build a whole structure, make
damn silly rules, wipe your arse with your left hand, make
love with your right. I mean, *really*! Why not *this* one for
your arse? And *this* one to make love with? Oh no. 'The
outsider,' they say, 'the outsider, of course, can never
understand.' They hug their misery and call it wisdom. And
that damned superiority. He has it. As if they all knew what
no one else knows. *He*—how could he, who's written so
brilliantly, how could he sit there and say all those damn
silly things?

(*He shakes his head.*)

I mean, it's just unforgivable.

ELAINE: Is it?

STEPHEN: Oh yes.

(*There's a pause.*)

ELAINE: (*Quietly*) And you're lonely.

STEPHEN: Sure.

(STEPHEN *smiles, as if conceding the true cause of his unhappiness. At this point, the lights in the scene begin to alter, focusing on the two characters, and the acting changes into something more heroic and heightened.*)

ELAINE: What's she like?

STEPHEN: She's very attractive. Her hair just falls, like this, across her face.

(ELAINE *nods slightly, tentatively.*)

ELAINE: If you want her, why not just ask her?

STEPHEN: Why is that not possible, do you suppose?

(*The lighting concentrates more, so we lose the space around them.*)

I've been here three days, watching her. Everything she does. Jazz. I know that much about her. I've discovered that she plays the jazz violin. But of course I did nothing about it. Then suddenly the Indian appears. Effortless.

ELAINE: You could have talked to her earlier.

STEPHEN: Yes. But I didn't. And now I feel the most terrible fool.

(ELAINE *looks at him, her acting expanding alarmingly.*)

ELAINE: Do it. Act. Seize her. Never nurse unrequited desire.

(*Music starts to play under this.*)

STEPHEN: You say that!

ELAINE: Yes. I've lived by it.

(*She gets up and, from the now-dark, great cries:*)

ANGELIS: Lights!

BOOM OPERATOR: Sound!

SOUND RECORDIST: Speed!

ANGELIS: Turn over!

CAMERAMAN: Rolling!

CLAPPERBOY: (*Doing so*) Mark it!

(*Brutes have illuminated the small acting area and a 35mm camera has circled round on a dolly with a* CREW, *while the sound men have edged on next to the action.* ELAINE *steps up*

25

into her highlight.)

ANGELIS: Action!

(ELAINE *continues in heightened but concentrated style. A close-up.*)

ELAINE: What do you think the purpose of life is? We could be giants. Simon, I swear it's the truth. This mess, this stew of unhappiness. How nobody dares to speak what they feel. There's something inside every human being, something suppressed. It's got to come out. I tell you, Simon, cut through to it. My friend, I beg you . . . let that something out.

(*The* DIRECTOR *now calls out*:)

ANGELIS: CUT!

(*The scene at once begins to fracture.*)

All right. Yes, print that.

(*Lights come on in the film studio as through the crowd comes a woman in her early thirties, well dressed in grey cotton trousers and a grey sweater. Her dark hair falls across her face. Her name is* PEGGY WHITTON, *and we are into* Scene Two.)

PEGGY: My God, it's terrible. That wasn't the point of the original scene.

ANGELIS: Please, yes, I am with you in a moment. I am most keen to hear what you say.

(*The* STEPHEN *actor stands at the edge of the set, peering out into the darkness.*)

STEPHEN: Is Paul there?

(*A* YOUNG MAN *has appeared. He is very good-looking in a white sailor suit. Meanwhile a* MAKE-UP GIRL *has come to deal with the* ELAINE *actress's face.*)

Paul.

PAUL: Hi. How are you?

MAKE-UP GIRL: All right, Monica?

ELAINE: Barbara, would you do my eyelashes?

MAKE-UP GIRL: Sure.

(STEPHEN *has kissed* PAUL *and is now sharing some strawberries* PAUL *has brought with him. A* PROPMAN *stands with more champagne, trying to find out whether he should refill the glasses. Another* PROPMAN *is unsure whether to take out the*

26

furniture.)

1ST PROPMAN: Do we take these?

2ND PROPMAN: Are we going back?

ANGELIS: I don't know.

CAMERAMAN: Do we need a re-set?

LOADER: Same shot?

(ANGELIS *at last raises his voice. He is a Greek in middle age, fat, wearing denim jeans and an overshirt in the style of Demis Roussos.*)

ANGELIS: Look, *please*, everyone, just give me a moment.

(STEPHEN *has begun to go, taking no notice.*)

STEPHEN: Angelis, d'you mind? I'm just slipping out. I'm just taking five minutes. I'll be in the dressing-room with Paul.

(*He and* PAUL *go. The* CLAPPERBOY *is eyeing* ANGELIS *beadily.*)

CLAPPERBOY: How long's he going to be?

PROPMAN: Are we going back?

ANGELIS: (*Shouts*) Look, just *hold* it.

(*At last everyone on the set is silent. Then, after a pause,* PEGGY *speaks very quietly*:)

PEGGY: You've quite destroyed Victor's writing, you know.

(ANGELIS *looks across, as if finally deciding he will need to deal with her.*)

SPARKS: Ten minutes, guv?

ANGELIS: Yes, OK.

(*There is a call from offstage*:)

FIRST ASSISTANT: Ten minutes! Ten minutes, everyone!

(*And at once the lights begin to go. Working lights high in the gantry go out.*)

PEGGY: It's the very essence of his writing that people never say what they feel. The woman's speech is completely ridiculous.

ANGELIS: You know, this isn't very easy for me.

PEGGY: No, but in the original novel . . .

(*The* ELAINE *actress is now left in another part of the studio with the* MAKE-UP *girl. Everyone else has gone.*)

ELAINE: Tell that prick I want him over here.

(ANGELIS *has heard this and is edging away from* PEGGY WHITTON, *for whom a canvas chair has been brought, in which she now sits.*)

PEGGY: Victor is a major, major writer.

ANGELIS: Sure.

(*He turns.*)

Coming.

ELAINE: I'm not acting with that man. He's doing whatever he can to upstage me. When we got to that bit about the United Nations, the failure of idealism speech . . .

ANGELIS: Sure.

ELAINE: . . . that faggot was wiggling his eyebrows.

ANGELIS: Yes, I know.

(*He shakes his head, the professional agreer.*)

It's really not good.

(PEGGY, *sitting by herself, now starts up again.*)

PEGGY: Jazz violinist! I was an actress!

ANGELIS: I know. Remember, we talked about the change.

PEGGY: Apart from anything, it's just so unlikely. All the jazz violinists you meet in Bombay.

ANGELIS: (*Reproachfully*) Peggy.

PEGGY: All right. It's not that, it's the *spirit*.

(*She looks at him, genuinely trying to find the right way of putting it.*)

Victor's work . . . I don't know how to say it . . . his prose is subtle. It's translucent. He makes you work to find out what's going on.

(*She stops, then starts again.*)

The best thing is, I shall tell you now what happened that day.

ANGELIS: Pardon. I am with you soon.

(*He turns back, conscious of* ELAINE *waiting ominously behind him.*)

ELAINE: I really want to talk.

ANGELIS: Please. I must speak to Peggy.

ELAINE: Why?

ANGELIS: I must. Without her agreement we have no film. It's just basic courtesy. For us it's a movie. For Peggy it's life.

(ELAINE'*s energy has blown itself out. Under her breath, therefore, and without malice*:)

ELAINE: Fuck Peggy.

ANGELIS: Yes, I know why you feel that.

ELAINE: It's spooky having her around.

ANGELIS: Please, she was so keen, really. It is the greatest compliment that she should come here and give us her time. To drive thirty miles from London. And she is only here for the day.

(*He is being charming.* ELAINE *looks at him without mercy.*)

If you would, I would be grateful.

ELAINE: All right. For now. But I'm not giving in.

(ELAINE *turns and goes out. There is a sudden silence. The whole crew has vanished inside a minute, and the previous chaotic scene has been wiped. Now* PEGGY *is sitting alone, trying to gather her thoughts, and* ANGELIS *is turning on the Bombay set, the only other person left under the working lights. When* PEGGY *finally speaks, she is struggling to put things clearly, searching for the truth in her own mind.*)

ANGELIS: Yes?

PEGGY: I didn't have any particular reason for choosing to go to that conference. It's clear in Victor's novel, I was staying in that hotel. I was in Bombay. I was making a film. At the time the Indian government wouldn't let American distributors take their profits out of the country, so there was a brief sort of fashion for using the rupees to make films over there. And this was some phoney sort of thriller, maharajahs and diamonds and so on. And I was basically a New York actress. Not even that. I was a philosophy major who worked in publishing. Someone wrote a play and asked me to act. And that's what I did. Easy America. The easiest place in the world.

(*She smiles.*)

So anyway this movie was dumb, it was long and dumb. I was off for a couple of days. Witty and literate people I was pretty short on, and I knew that at least if I went along to this conference I'd read about in the papers . . . well, the great thing would be not to have to talk about films. I had briefly met, I guess for ten minutes maybe, this young Englishman, who in your version, is rather a bore. But that's not how he was. In person he was very . . . *charming* . . .

29

BIRKBECK
LIBRARY
COLLEGE

suddenly gives up the struggle.)

Look, fuck it, I don't know.

ANGELIS: No, go on.

PEGGY: I mean, it's pointless even telling you this because you need a writer, you know?

ANGELIS: I know.

(PEGGY *looks at him seriously.*)

PEGGY: Angelis, you could understand everything and still not be able to show it. That's what writers do. They make you see it, and on this film you don't have one.

(*She shakes her head.*)

Elaine, for instance. I mean, she wasn't direct like that. Not Elaine. She always just insinuated. She was always just there.

ANGELIS: Did she . . .?

PEGGY: (*With affection*) Oh, and she was warm!

ANGELIS: (*Hurt*) She's warm in this.

PEGGY: She's understanding, yes.

ANGELIS: She's one of the characters the writer's done best.

(PEGGY *looks at him, as if realizing how deep the gulf of misunderstanding is between them. So it is kindly, as to an invalid, that she now speaks.*)

PEGGY: Please, do you think . . . could you get me a glass of water?

ANGELIS: Yes. I'll get someone . . .

PEGGY: No, if . . . you could get it yourself. Just to give me a moment. A moment's clarity.

(*She smiles to try and take the offence out of the request. They look at each other, both still, she being gracious.*)

I know it's expensive. But I just need a moment alone.

(*There's a pause. Then he turns and goes out.* PEGGY *stands alone on the deserted set, which is ghostly in the working light. She turns and speaks straight out to the audience.*)

Young. I know how I smelt then. Young. Unmistakably young. Not even sure or confident, but irreplaceably, indecently young. You never get it back. How can you? Oh, God. Nothing makes sense, none of it, unless you understand this one basic fact. How do I put it?

(*She smiles.*)

That I was so young.

(*From the back of the area* VICTOR MEHTA *is appearing,
trailed by a group of men in suits. As they cross the stage in
animated argument, the* CREW *appear and transform the set as
they come, turning it from the hotel lobby into a modern
conference room. This is as sketchily marked as the original
set, for it consists of twenty chairs at seemingly random angles
on a yet larger expanse of floor. Other elements are minimal.*)

MARTINSON: Mr Mehta, please, I must insist. You must listen to
what I have to say. It is a simple statement. Really, Mr
Mehta, you cannot refuse.

(*The lights change.* PEGGY *moves into the newly assembled set,
and* MEHTA *appears, answering vigorously.*)

MEHTA: You ask me to accept this. I cannot accept it. It's out of
the question, I'm afraid. I'm a free writer. All my work has
been about freedom. Now you ask me to abandon it. No!

(PEGGY *smiles across the room at him, and* Scene Three *has
begun.*)

PEGGY: Victor . . .

MEHTA: Peggy, I am sorry. I had hoped to have lunch with you.
Now it is impossible. There is trouble.

PEGGY: What kind?

MEHTA: This here is Mr Martinson. He is running the conference.
He is the man who invited me to speak.

(*He gestures at* MARTINSON, *who is standing at the centre of a
group of suited diplomats.* MARTINSON *is a tall, grave and
persistent Swede, whose apparent doggedness turns out to have
an iron quality. He is in his forties.*)

You remember last night . . .

PEGGY: Yes.

MEHTA: . . . after our dinner . . . I told you something here made
me uneasy from the start . . .

PEGGY: You enjoyed dinner.

MEHTA: Yes.

(*He pauses, thrown by this apparent irrelevance, then persists:*)
Yes, I did at the time. But that was last night. And now
this morning Mr Martinson has come with this evil news.

MARTINSON: Perhaps, perhaps if I were allowed to repeat it to
    your friend . . .

MEHTA: Miss Whitton . . .

MARTINSON: . . . she might be able to judge more dispassionately
    how serious it is.

    (*A pause.* MEHTA *nods.*)

MEHTA: Very well.

    (MARTINSON *turns patiently to* PEGGY.)

MARTINSON: There has been an approach from the Mozambique
    delegation . . .

MEHTA: Mozambique!

MARTINSON: Yes. You said.

MEHTA: There is no such place. It is merely a province of China.

MARTINSON: I am not sure they would necessarily agree.

MEHTA: They are a tongue only. Not even a puppet. They are
    simply another man's mouth.

    (MARTINSON *turns back, apparently almost indifferent.*)

MARTINSON: Well, it is not really central . . .

MEHTA: It is very 'central'.

MARTINSON: (*Ignoring him*) Well, it is not really the point. There
    is a faction, let us say it, from the socialist countries . . .

MEHTA: I . . .

MARTINSON: (*Holding up a hand to silence him*) Yes. From
    whatever direction . . . that objects to Mr Mehta's presence
    at the conference. Because of some things he's written in the
    past.

    (MEHTA, *justified, looks to* PEGGY *for her reaction.*)

MEHTA: You see!

PEGGY: Well, there are some people—

MEHTA: Of course, you are right.

PEGGY: . . . factions that are bound to object to some of Victor's
    books. I mean, I've only read a couple—sorry, Victor—but
    what he says doesn't seem to me to read like hostility. He
    loves the countries; he attacks the regimes. Surely even they
    can see there's a difference.

MARTINSON: Yes. But they do dislike the implication in some of
    the novels that anyone who professes Marxist ideas
    necessarily does so as justification for whatever terror he

wants to commit.

MEHTA: It's true.

MARTINSON: There's a phrase where you call Marxism
'dictatorship's fashionable dress'.

(MARTINSON *smiles lightly.*)

Well, they do find that peculiarly insulting.

PEGGY: Yes. But surely they knew that in advance?

MARTINSON: It still causes great anger.

PEGGY: It can't be overnight they've started to read.

(*There is a momentary pause as* PEGGY *waits for the
explanation.*)

So? What are they suggesting? Are you trying to say he's
not allowed to speak?

MARTINSON: No, no, goodness, Miss Whitton . . .

(*He turns round and smiles at the* DIPLOMATS, *who smile and
shake their heads.*)

DIPLOMATS: No, goodness, no . . .

MARTINSON: No one is suggesting . . . I think that would be
terrible. Censorship is something we do not countenance at
all.

MEHTA: Oh, really?

MARTINSON: No.

(PEGGY *frowns, still not understanding.*)

PEGGY: So?

(MARTINSON *has already begun to take a slip of paper from his
pocket.*)

MARTINSON: A preliminary statement.

MEHTA: You see!

MARTINSON: That is the suggestion.

PEGGY: What about?

MARTINSON: Well . . .

PEGGY: Is that it there?

MARTINSON: Yes.

(*He has unfolded it, white, neat, a single page.*)

It's been drafted by a committee, just a short statement,
that is all.

PEGGY: Saying what?

MARTINSON: Mr Mehta would read it before going on to give his own talk.

PEGGY: But what does it say?

MARTINSON: It's about the nature of fiction.

(*He smiles slightly again, the quiet incendiarist.*)

I suppose it argues all fiction is lies.

(PEGGY *reacts in disbelief.*)

PEGGY: Oh, my God . . . no, I don't believe it . . .

MEHTA: Didn't I say?

MARTINSON: Please.

PEGGY: It is ludicrous.

MARTINSON: No.

(PEGGY *looks at him, lost for a response.*)

PEGGY: How long?

MARTINSON: It's brief. As I say, Mr Mehta would read it out before his address, then he would be free to go on and say whatever he likes.

(PEGGY *is about to react, but* MARTINSON *carries on, suddenly on the offensive.*)

Please. I don't like it. I am not easy at suggesting it. It is not the ideal procedure at all. However, bear in mind I am pleading for the survival of my conference. This seems to me a small price to pay.

MEHTA: I don't accept that.

(MARTINSON *looks at him, authoritative.*)

MARTINSON: We are here to discuss world poverty. The conference has taken many years to assemble, and in a week's time, the reluctant governments of the West will return home and try to forget they have ever attended. It is true. Any excuse they can find to dismiss the whole occasion as a shambles they will seize on and exploit. Therefore it is, without question, essential that the conference is given every chance of life, every chance of success. If Mr Mehta refuses to read out this little concoction, then he will make a fine gesture of individual conscience against the pressures—I will say this and please do not repeat it—of less than scrupulous groups, and he will go home to Shropshire, and he will feel proud and clever and generally excellent. And *Time* magazine will write of him, yes, and there will be editorials and the bloody writer's freedom, hurrah! But the conference will have been destroyed. It is a short statement, it is an unimportant statement, because it is on a subject which is of no conceivable general interest or importance, namely, what a novel is, which I can hardly see is a subject of vital and continuing fascination to the poor. Frankly, who cares? is my attitude, and I think you will find it is the attitude of all the non-aligned countries . . .

(*He looks behind him for confirmation, and the* DIPLOMATS *all nod.*)

Certainly, the Scandinavian bloc . . .

DIPLOMATS: Yes . . . Indeed, it is our attitude.

MARTINSON: What is your phrase? We do not give a toss what a novel is. I think I may even say this is Scandinavia's official position, and if a man stands up at the beginning of this morning's session and lies about what a novel is, I will just be grateful because then there is a better chance that aid will flow, because grain will flow, because water will flow . . .

MEHTA: This is blackmail!

MARTINSON: No.

MEHTA: Exploitation of our feelings of guilt! The West is guilty, and so it must pay a price in lies!

PEGGY: The West?

MEHTA: Drag us down to their standards!

(*He has got up and is now standing in animated argument with himself.*)

No, it is wrong!

(MARTINSON *turns coolly to* PEGGY.)

MARTINSON: Miss Whitton?

(*She has been sitting quietly through* MARTINSON'*s explanation.*)

PEGGY: (*Very casually*) Well, I mean, we should hear it, shouldn't we?

MEHTA: What?

PEGGY: The statement.

(PEGGY *turns to* MEHTA.)

Have you read it?

35

MEHTA: Are you mad? I did not write it, therefore I shall not read it.

PEGGY: (*To* MARTINSON) Read it.

(*Then, before* MEHTA *can interrupt.*)

Victor. Last night, when we went upstairs—

MEHTA: Yes, all right, thank you . . .

PEGGY: . . . to the *bedroom* . . .

(*She then turns and flashes a smile at* MARTINSON.)

We only met last night.

(MEHTA *looks at her beadily. Then, with bitter quiet:*)

MEHTA: All right. Very well, yes, let us hear it. Thank you, Peggy.

(*He sits down to listen.* PEGGY *smiles.* MARTINSON *begins very formally.*)

MARTINSON: 'Fiction, by its very nature, distorts and misrepresents reality, so in a way a man who stands before you as a writer of fiction, as I do today, is already some way towards admitting that as a historical witness he is unreliable—

(MEHTA *gets up, exploding.*)

MEHTA: No, no, no, no! It is not to be endured.

PEGGY: Victor . . .

MEHTA: It is Nazi.

PEGGY: It is not Nazi.

MEHTA: It is Nazi.

(*For the first time* PEGGY *begins to start taking enthusiastic part in the argument, enjoying herself.*)

PEGGY: 'Nazi' means 'National Socialist'. This is not National Socialist. It is not German propaganda of the thirties.

MEHTA: It is neo-Nazi.

PEGGY: No, it is a serious proposition . . .

MEHTA: Nonsense.

PEGGY: . . . to which we may listen rationally and calmly and as adults and say, 'Yes, mmm, this is so, this is not so.' Let us therefore . . .

MEHTA: (*Darkly*) This woman is driving me crazy.

PEGGY: . . . exercise our minds and address the real, the central problem of the day, which is: is all fiction distortion? Come

on, let's examine this. I did a term paper. What do we mean
by distortion? Are these good arguments on this piece of
paper or are they bad?

MEHTA: Not enough the moral blackmail of the Third World,
but now there is sexual blackmail. A poor man who
stumbles into a bed . . .
(*He turns to explain to* MARTINSON.)
I have slept with this woman last night; this woman I have
embraced . . .

PEGGY: (*Delighted, pretending shock*) Really, Victor, you mustn't—
you, a gentleman—disclose to the entire UNESCO
Secretariat . . .

MEHTA: I approach this woman, a dinner with friends, a
conversation about Greek history, an understanding as
between strangers that they will spend a night . . . a
civilized arrangement . . .

PEGGY: (*Smiles*) Yes.

MEHTA: . . . and now she must betray me.
(PEGGY *smiles at him warmly, her mischievousness past.*)

PEGGY: Nobody betrays you, Victor. Perhaps Martinson is right.
That in the scale of things this doesn't matter very much.
(*There is a pause as* MEHTA *stands alone, touched. Then he
nods.*)

MEHTA: Bring me the man who has written this. I will negotiate.
(*At the back one of the* DIPLOMATS *goes out.*)
I do this because she is beautiful. No other reason, yes? Why
did Victor Mehta read the statement on the nature of fiction
at the UNESCO conference in Bombay in 1976? For thighs.
For thighs and arms, and hair that falls across the face.
(*At once* STEPHEN ANDREWS *comes in, smiling, talking to the*
DIPLOMAT. *He is followed by* M'BENGUE, *a Senegalese in his
thirties, small, bright, elegant.* STEPHEN *is gracious, but
pleased.*)

STEPHEN: Ah, well, this is excellent!

PEGGY: Stephen!

STEPHEN: I hear there is to be a climb-down. Thank goodness.
The whole conference endangered, I heard . . .

MEHTA: What? Is it him?

37

STEPHEN: For something so petty, so meaningless . . .

MEHTA: (*Quietly*) Peggy . . .

PEGGY: I didn't know!

STEPHEN: This is my friend M. M'Bengue of Senegal. He helped us draft . . .

MEHTA: Then I will not read it. No, if it is Mr Andrews . . .
(*He turns away.* STEPHEN *smiles.*)

STEPHEN: . . . these few remarks.
(*Between them* MARTINSON *looks puzzled.*)

MARTINSON: Are you old enemies?

MEHTA: No. Last night he insulted me on my arrival here, and now I see, yes, it is because of Peggy, because he was to eat dinner with her. That is the motive behind this fine display of principle. She stood him up to eat with me.

PEGGY: (*Looks down*) Oh, lord.
(MARTINSON *is still frowning.*)

MARTINSON: Well, this does not mean . . . surely the person must be separate from the argument?

MEHTA: No.

MARTINSON: The motive for the argument does not affect its validity. As Miss Whitton said, a thing is true or untrue, worth proposing or not worth proposing . . .

MEHTA: No!

MARTINSON: . . . no matter who proposes it. As, for instance, as one might say of Hitler's love of Wagner . . .

PEGGY: (*Groaning*) Oh, my God . . .

MARTINSON: . . . does not mean . . .

MEHTA: Let us not . . .

MARTINSON: . . . that Wagner's music is discredited . . .
(*The* DIPLOMATS *shake their heads in agreement.*)

MEHTA: No.

PEGGY: *Please.*

MARTINSON: And so it is for whatever . . . I cannot say this well . . .

MEHTA: Indeed.

MARTINSON: . . . reason it is that he comes . . .

MEHTA: (*Exasperated at* MARTINSON'*s dogged logic*) But *you* said, you yourself said, *less* than scrupulous groups were *using* this argument to threaten . . .

MARTINSON: But *you*, Mr Mehta, your motives. Only a moment
ago you were saying it was not for principle that *you* would
speak; it was for thighs.

M'BENGUE: (*To* STEPHEN) Thighs?

MEHTA: I would give in, yes. Then. But now I will not give in. I
am shaken awake.

(ELAINE *comes in, very cheerful.*)

ELAINE: Hey, I hear this is getting very interesting.

MARTINSON: I'm not sure.

MEHTA: (*At once*) Please, no, nothing now, not in front of the
press . . .

MARTINSON: Miss le Fanu. I think . . .

ELAINE: Off the record?

(MARTINSON *looks across to* MEHTA, *who nods.*)

MEHTA: All right.

(MARTINSON *takes advantage of the moment to reassert his
chairmanship.*)

MARTINSON: Let us please to put motive aside. Let us examine
the true reason for the dispute. You agree?

(MEHTA *looks at him without enthusiasm, but he goes on.*)
Let us try to understand the feelings of the African
countries in particular. Well, M. M'Bengue can explain.

(*There is a pause. The others look to* M'BENGUE.)

M'BENGUE: It is true that we have chosen you, Mr Mehta, and it
is to a degree arbitrary. There is a greater argument and we
are using you as an instrument merely to draw attention to
it. It happens that your novels are full of the most
provocative observations—I will not linger on them. In
particular, what you say of Madame Mao . . .

MARTINSON: (*Panicking*) Oh no.

MEHTA: (*With renewed vigour*) Ah well, yes.

M'BENGUE: You lack respect . . .

MEHTA: You ask me to desist from writing of Madame Mao?

M'BENGUE: No.

MEHTA: I cannot. I am a comic novelist. It would be superhuman
to refrain . . .

MARTINSON: It is not the point.

39

MEHTA: You ask me to refrain from writing of a woman who does not dare make public the date of her birthday because she is frightened it will *over-excite the masses*?

(*He stares insanely at* M'BENGUE.)

She is a gift. You ask me not to write of her?

MARTINSON: (*Quietly leading* M'BENGUE *back*) The greater argument, M. M'Bengue, please.

STEPHEN: Go on.

M'BENGUE: Very well, it is this. We take aid from the West because we are poor, and in everything we are made to feel our inferiority. The price you ask us to pay is not money but misrepresentation. The way the nations of the West make us pay is by representing us continually in their organs of publicity as bunglers and murderers and fools. I have spent time in England and there the yellow press does not speak of Africa except to report how a nun has been raped, or there has been a tribal massacre, or how we are slaughtering the elephants—the elephants who are so much more suitable for television programmes than the Africans— or how corrupt and incompetent such-and-such a government is. If the crop succeeds, it is not news. If we build a dam, it is called boring. 'Oh, we do not report the building of dams,' say your newspapers. Dam-building is dull. Boring. The white man's word for everything to which he does not wish to come to terms. Yes, he will give us money, but the price we will pay is that he will not seek to understand our point of view. Pro-Moscow, pro-Washington, that is the only way you can see the world. All your terms are political, and your politics is the crude fight between your two great blocs. Is Angola pro-Russian? Is it pro-American? These are the only questions you ever ask yourselves. As if the whole world could be seen in those terms. In your terms. In the white man's terms and through the white man's media.

(*He looks down, as if to hide the strength of feeling behind what he says.*)

And so it hurts . . . it begins to hurt that the context of the struggle in Africa is never made clear. It is never explained.

40

Your news agencies report *our* events, and from a point of view which is eccentric and sensational. All this, day in, day out, we endure and make no protest, and when we come to take part in this conference in Bombay, we find that UNESCO has invited a particular keynote speaker—a black man himself, though of course, because he is Indian, it is not how he sees himself: he thinks himself superior to the black man from the bush—a speaker whose reputation is for wit at the expense of others, whose reporting is not positive, so of course he is called a hero in the West. He is called a bringer of truths because he seeks to discredit those who struggle. And so it is true, yes, in the middle of the night, Mr Andrews and I, walking to the Gate of India, did say: the greater, the larger misrepresentation we can do nothing about—those who control the money will control the information—but the lesser one, yes, and tonight. A stand is possible.

(*He turns to* MEHTA.)

You distort things in your novels because it is funny to distort, because indeed the surface of things *is* funny, if you do not understand how that surface comes to be, if you do not look underneath. Just as a funeral may be funny to a small boy who sees it passing in the street and does not know the man who is dead. So also no doubt in Africa it is superficially funny to see us blundering about. But who makes the jokes? The rich nations.

MEHTA: No.

M'BENGUE: Jokes, Mr Mehta, are a product of security. If one is secure, one may laugh at others. Even—this is the really telling thing—one may laugh at oneself. 'Look at my little heap, ha ha,' the white man says, knowing full well it is a big heap. I may pretend to be low by joking, by making jokes about myself, which are really a way of saying I am so high I don't have to care. I can say anything. That is the truth. Humour, like everything, is something you buy. Free speech? Buy. But what is this freedom? The luxury of the rich who are sure of what they have.

(MEHTA *just looks at him.*)

41

MEHTA: (*Quietly*) What would you do? Ban it?

M'BENGUE: No. I would ask that black men who ascend from their countries do not conspire in the humiliation of those they have left behind.

(*There is a pause. When* MEHTA *replies it is with a gravity which matches* M'BENGUE'*s.*)

MEHTA: People are venal and stupid and corrupt, no more so now than at any other time in history. They tell themselves lies. The writer asks no more than the right to point those lies out. What you say of how the press sees you is probably true, and the greater grievance you have I am sure is right. But I will not add to the lies.

(*There is a pause. And then he gets up.*)

And that is all I have to say.

PEGGY: Victor . . .

MEHTA: No.

(PEGGY *speaks, knowing what she says is not true.*)

PEGGY: It's just silly. It's a silly argument.

(MEHTA *goes out. The whole group is suspended for a moment, then* M'BENGUE *gets up and leaves at the other side.*
MARTINSON *looks behind him to one of his* AIDES.)

MARTINSON: The educational motion from tomorrow's agenda . . .

AIDE: Yes.

MARTINSON: We may move it to today?

AIDE: It's possible.

MARTINSON: Delay Mr Mehta's address until tomorrow. If that's agreeable?

(*He looks to* STEPHEN.)

STEPHEN: Yes.

MARTINSON: Mr Andrews, you will give us twenty-four hours?

STEPHEN: (*Conscious of* PEGGY'*s gaze*) Of course.

(MARTINSON *gets up and leads his team out silently.* ELAINE, PEGGY *and* STEPHEN *are left alone.*)

PEGGY: Let me talk to Stephen.

ELAINE: Should I stay?

PEGGY: Yes. So that it's clear. So there's a witness.

(*She gets up.*)

Yes.

(*She crosses the room and stands a moment, looking out.*)
It's hot.
(*Then, characteristically, she starts a seemingly new subject, from nowhere.*)
In Westchester County, where I was brought up, I went with the boys who asked me—always—because . . . well . . . the men who have the courage to ask a girl who's at all independent are a sort of . . . self-selecting élite who *deserve* to sleep with the girls who are at all independent, if you see what I mean. But the moment they got serious I'd say, 'Why?' Because what's the point?
(*She turns to* ELAINE.)
Elaine will understand.

ELAINE: (*Smiling*) Yes.

(*Then* PEGGY *turns back to* STEPHEN.)

PEGGY: You've not been in America?

STEPHEN: No.

PEGGY: It's this feeling of choice you have, that it almost doesn't matter who's in the cut-off Levis or, for that matter, in the button-down shirt. I mean relationships—*why*? What's the need? You understand?

(STEPHEN *does not react.*)

They're just trouble. And . . . well . . . when I was sixteen, I made a resolution. I had a girlfriend. We were walking in the Rockies, and the view, I can tell you, was something as you came over to Boulder, Colorado. And we had a six-pack right there on top of the mountain. And she was a *good* girl, I mean a really good girl, you could trust your life to her. And we said: let's not ever mess with the bad things at all.

STEPHEN: Goodness.

PEGGY: I mean, we don't need to. So let's not.

(*There's a pause.*)

Now, what's sad is I saw her six months ago. She's married to a lawyer in DC, and he's never there, he's out over-achieving all day, and she doesn't like him when he is there, and so she's fucking around, so that one day, she told me, she got this *pain*, this really terrible pain *here*, you know? She panicked. She was really desperate. Into

43

hospital. She told me for the first time in her life she prayed. Right there, in Emergency. And I said, 'Really, what was your prayer, Elise?' And she said she prayed, 'Oh God, let it not be cervical cancer. God, please. God, just do this for me. If it's not cancer, I swear I'll never cheat on Arnold again. And *that* . . .

(*She laughs delightedly.*)

. . . I tell you *that*, when I come to write my novel about America, that will be its title: *Cheating on Arnold*. That will be its name. Because, you see, that is *not* what is going to happen to me. You understand? Because there is no need.

(*She says this with the complete conviction of youth. Then smiles.*)

Now the two of you, Victor, you, both slightly ridiculous, slightly contemptible, in my view, you see? Elaine will agree. That sort of behaviour, men being jealous, men fighting, it's out of date. Outdated, Stephen. Unnecessary, Stephen. I mean, drop the bad behaviour and you might get somewhere.

STEPHEN: Meaning I will get somewhere?

PEGGY: Drop the bad behaviour and you will get somewhere.

(*A silence while this sinks in.* ELAINE *looks down, amused.*
STEPHEN *cautious, but enjoying his power.*)

STEPHEN: That's kind of you, but the fact is, I didn't act alone.

PEGGY: Ah, well.

STEPHEN: There's a committee.

PEGGY: (*Vigorously*) Well, I'm not offering *all* of them.

(ELAINE *smiles.*)

Even Westchester County has its limits, you know.

STEPHEN: Yes, but there are other people, and they do have views.

PEGGY: They can be swung.

STEPHEN: Because they're black?

(PEGGY *looks at him with contempt.*)

PEGGY: That's when you're really boring, Stephen. The sex drops off you. It's like your prick drops off when you say things like that.

STEPHEN: All right.

PEGGY: No, not because they're black, you wimp, but because it's a committee of—how many?

STEPHEN: Four.

PEGGY: Right. And you're on it, that's all. And when you're not apologizing for your own existence, you can actually be quite a plausible human being.

(STEPHEN *looks at her, touched.*)

STEPHEN: Weren't you *moved* by what M'Bengue said just now?

PEGGY: Stephen, whose cause does he damage by stopping the conference?

STEPHEN: He doesn't want to stop the conference.

PEGGY: His own.

STEPHEN: But . . .

PEGGY: Senegal's. Somalia's. Mozambique's.

STEPHEN: But if Victor could be persuaded . . .

PEGGY: Victor was persuaded. Until you appeared.

(*There's a pause. Then* PEGGY *turns, as if finally despairing.*)
All right, then, make your little stand . . .

STEPHEN: It's not that.

PEGGY: . . . whatever it is. No one will remember.

STEPHEN: It's principle.

PEGGY: Principle, indeed! People do what they want to, then afterwards, if it suits them, they call it principle.

STEPHEN: No.

PEGGY: Rationalization of what you've already decided, that's what principle is.

(STEPHEN *is already shaking his head.*)

STEPHEN: Certain things are important. Certain things are *good.*

PEGGY: How can you say, you who are not involved? M'Bengue, sure, he's a member of a government . . .

STEPHEN: He's a civil servant.

PEGGY: All right, he's a civil servant who represents a government which stands to gain from the successful outcome of this conference—so when *he* says 'principle', we listen. It's at some cost. It's at some personal expense. But your principles have been bought in the store on the corner and cost you nothing.

(STEPHEN *looks down, very hurt.*)

45

STEPHEN: No, well, I'm sorry . . .

PEGGY: Look, Stephen, I don't mean to be unkind to you. I like you.

ELAINE: (*Smiles*) She does.

PEGGY: You attract unkindness because so often you're not *you*. You're this ragbag of opinions.

STEPHEN: So are you.

(PEGGY *looks at him, surprised, not understanding.*)

How is it different? Your freedom you've just told us about, your sexual freedom, what's that if not some contrived and idiotic idea based on some mountaintop experience you've talked yourself into believing was a revelation? And a revelation meaning what? That you may sleep with anyone and not get involved. Gosh, well, thank goodness. What a convenient discovery. Remind me to buy climbing boots next time I'm out.

ELAINE: Stephen . . .

STEPHEN: The six-pack philosopher. Really! Entitled to patronize. And from what position? From the safety of beauty. From the absolute safety of being beautiful.

(*He stops, aware of having hurt her. He begins to apologize.*)

Well, I'm sorry. Something happened to me last night, while you were no doubt with . . .

PEGGY: Victor.

STEPHEN: Quite. I walked to the Gateway of India with M'Bengue, among the small kerosene stoves, suffocating, the heat, the dope, tripping against beggars, watching boys of ten and eleven with fat joints stuck in their mouths. We walked along Chowpatty Beach, and I listened to a man trying to explain to me what it's like to see the world the other way up. To come—can you imagine?—from Dakar, to fly through the night and arrive in this conference hall to listen to the well-heeled agents of the West argue that of course aid never gets through, and, when it gets through, how officials rip it off. And how really all it does is create a disease called aid dependency. Aid doesn't really help, the West keeps saying, to salve its own bloated conscience. Yes, I do feel these things, these things that seem to you

46

affectations only because to believe in *anything* now in the West, except money or sex or motor cars, is to mark yourself out as foolish. A subject for satire. At which Victor Mehta is adept.

(*There is a pause.* PEGGY *looks at him, lost.* ELAINE *then suddenly:*)

ELAINE: Then argue it out.

STEPHEN: What?

ELAINE: The two of you. Just the two of you. Argue it out.

STEPHEN: He won't listen.

ELAINE: He'll listen.

(*She looks across to where* PEGGY *stands alone, at the side.*)

If Peggy says.

(*There is a pause. Then* PEGGY *turns and nods slightly.*)

STEPHEN: All right. This evening.

ELAINE: Yes.

PEGGY: Elaine can adjudicate.

STEPHEN: Good.

PEGGY: She will decide.

(*She smiles.*)

And whoever wins, wins me.

STEPHEN: No!

PEGGY: Yes! Yes! *That* will be principle. That's principle—having something to lose.

STEPHEN: No!

PEGGY: Freedom!

STEPHEN: That's not freedom. My God, that's bartering.

(PEGGY *has already started to gather her things up as if it were settled.*)

PEGGY: Elaine?

STEPHEN: It's sick.

ELAINE: (*Drily*) Putting her body where her mouth is—how can that be wrong?

(STEPHEN *stands as* ELAINE *gets up to go as well.*)

STEPHEN: It's impossible. What will I say to M'Bengue? 'I'm sorry, we have to give way to this offensive Indian because last night . . .' No, it's ridiculous.

PEGGY: Yes. If you lose. If you win . . .

(*She smiles, leaving the rest unsaid.*)
If you're right after all, if Victor is wrong to say all these
things . . .

STEPHEN: He is.

PEGGY: Very well then. Argue, Stephen. If you want me, argue
it tonight.

(*She goes out.* ELAINE *and* STEPHEN *are left alone.*)

STEPHEN: Oh, God. Elaine . . .

(ELAINE *looks at him affectionately.*)

ELAINE: There's so much passion in you, so much emotion, all
the time. This is wrong, that's wrong. Well, tonight you will
get the chance to direct that emotion, and in a good cause.
(*A pause.*)
What better cause than Peggy Whitton, eh?
(*There is a moment of warmth between them. Suddenly they
both smile at the shared ludicrousness of the situation.*)
Come on, I'll buy you lunch.
(*And at once* ANGELIS *appears from the back of the stage,
walking on to the set and calling to his unseen followers.
This time the two scenes interweave, one group of people
walking right through the other,* Scene Three *oblivious of*
Scene Four's *existence.*)

ANGELIS: Lunch, everyone.

(ELAINE *and* STEPHEN *are still standing looking at each other.*)

ELAINE: I'm fond of you. You're a fool, and I'm fond of you.

(*An* ASSISTANT *has carried on a chair for* ANGELIS's *approval.*)

ANGELIS: Strike the set!

ASSISTANT: Is this the right kind of chair for the bedroom, Mr
Angelis?

ANGELIS: Yes, that's fine.

ASSISTANT: They want you to look at the bed.

(ELAINE *and* STEPHEN *are replacing their chairs as
simultaneously the* CREW *have appeared and are taking all the
chairs off, clearing the set.*)

ELAINE: Where shall we eat?

ANGELIS: I will look at the bed later. The bed comes later.

STEPHEN: I want to go to the Temple of the Janes. Have you been
there?

48

ELAINE: No.

STEPHEN: I hear it's beautiful.

(*The* ASSISTANT *persists as* ANGELIS *watches the* CREW *at work.*)

ASSISTANT: If you could . . . Will it be soft or hard?

ANGELIS: Soft.

ASSISTANT: What colour?

ANGELIS: Blue. Blue spread.

ASSISTANT: (*Frowns*) Really?

(ELAINE *has taken* STEPHEN'*s arm.*)

ELAINE: And let's go to Doongarwadi, to the Parsee funeral ground.

STEPHEN: Is that where the vultures pick at the bodies of the dead?

ELAINE: That's the one.

STEPHEN: Good. Let's go there.

(*The lights lose them as they go.*)

Lunch before?

ELAINE: After, I think.

(*They're gone.*)

ANGELIS: (*Panicking now*) White. Oh, God. I don't know. White sheets, white spread too. Sure. What the hell? Who cares? Get the book.

ASSISTANT: The book says white.

ANGELIS: Then white. If it's in the book, it must be right.

(*The set has been cleared. There is only an empty floor.* PEGGY WHITTON *runs on, as if the set were still there. She doesn't realize* STEPHEN *and* ELAINE *have gone.*)

PEGGY: Stephen! Victor agrees. It's on.

(*She stands, triumphant.* ANGELIS *does not see or hear her.*)

ANGELIS: I'm bored.

(*A great cry.*)

Lunch! Lunch!

ACT TWO

At the end of the interval, in the darkness we hear a recording of PEGGY's *letter home.*

PEGGY: Dear Sue: Alone but not lonely in Bombay. I have met a man—I cannot tell you—I have met a novelist, Victor Mehta. A man of great gracefulness. Difficult, of course, like the best men. And very proud. In a fit of stupidity, I have agreed—oh, God, how I agreed this I have no idea—I have agreed to sleep with the winner of an argument. One of the men is Victor. The other . . . not.

Scene Five. *The film studio. There is now a bedroom, which is represented by a bed and a wall behind with a door in it, which leads off to an imaginary bathroom. The room is unnaturally spacious, occupying a large area, detailed but incomplete.*

Dotted near it are canvas chairs and camera equipment, though the camera itself is missing. The actors are sitting about in casual clothes, waiting for rehearsal. They are not yet in costume. The ELAINE *actress is sitting at one side by herself with a magazine. The* MARTINSON *actor is doing* The Times *crossword. He was born an Englishman, but is now a self-consciously international figure in blue jeans, gold medallion and muted Californian T-shirt. The* M'BENGUE *actor stands in the middle, quite still, looking off into the distance.*

M'BENGUE: Well, what is happening?

MARTINSON: I don't know.

(*He frowns.*)

What on earth could be one . . . two . . . three . . . four . . . five . . . six . . . seven letters, begins with Z, and the clue is 'It's the plague of the earth'?

ELAINE: Zionism.

MARTINSON: What?

(*The* PEGGY *actress comes on. She is wearing a band round her head, to push her hair back. She has a dressing-gown on over her shirt and trousers.*)

PEGGY: Has anyone seen Angelis?

ELAINE: No. We're all called, but there's nobody here.

(MARTINSON *is staring at* ELAINE *in disbelief.*)

MARTINSON: What d'you mean, 'Zionism'?

ELAINE: Well, it's seven letters, beginning with Z.

MARTINSON: But are you . . .

ELAINE: What?

MARTINSON: . . . just saying it because it's a word?

ELAINE: It's a word.

MARTINSON: I know it's a word.

(*He pauses.*)

I know it's a word.

ELAINE: It's got seven letters and it begins with Z.

(PEGGY *has stood a moment, taking no notice, and now smiles round.*)

PEGGY: I want to show you various dressing-gowns and then you can say what's best for the scene, OK?

(*She disappears through the door in the set and closes it. From the side the* STEPHEN *actor appears, in loose grey flannels and pullover, with a book. He is a pleasant and easy-going man. He sits.*)

STEPHEN: Hello.

MARTINSON: But are you also saying it's the plague of the earth?

ELAINE: What?

MARTINSON: Zionism.

ELAINE: (*Frowns*) Well, I don't think it's a very good thing, if that's what you mean.

(*She goes back to reading, but* MARTINSON *looks round to see who else is taking notice, then persists.*)

MARTINSON: No, that's not actually what I mean. What I mean is, are you actually suggesting that Zionism is the plague of the earth?

ELAINE: Well, obviously, if it's got seven letters and begins with Z, it scarcely matters what I think about it. What matters is

51

BIRKBECK
LIBRARY
COLLEGE

what the compiler thinks, and obviously, I don't know, perhaps *The Times* has Arab crossword compilers these days. Perhaps they have some Libyan on the staff.

MARTINSON: I suppose you think that's funny.

ELAINE: No, I don't think it's funny. I'm just saying . . .

(PEGGY *has come through the bathroom door in a blue-and-white spotted dressing-gown.*)

PEGGY: Well, what d'you think?

MARTINSON: Very nice.

PEGGY: Monica?

ELAINE: Fine.

STEPHEN: (*Looking up*) Honestly, it's fine.

(PEGGY *goes out smiling.* MARTINSON *is still waiting.*)

MARTINSON: Are you seriously saying . . .

ELAINE: I'm not saying anything.

MARTINSON: You actually think *The Times* would employ somebody . . .?

ELAINE: No.

MARTINSON: Do you know the history of the state of Palestine?

ELAINE: Well, as a matter of fact, yes, I do.

MARTINSON: Do you know what happened to the Jews between 1939 and 1945?

ELAINE: Yes, I do. They got wiped out.

MARTINSON: It's not *funny*.

ELAINE: I know it's not funny, for Christ's sake. I am not for one second saying it *is* funny. It's you that seems determined to take issue with everything I say.

MARTINSON: I'm not.

ELAINE: It's just . . . objectively . . . it seems a remarkable fact that a people who once enjoyed the sympathy of the whole world for what they had suffered have, in the space of just thirty-five years, managed to *squander* that sympathy by creating a vicious, narrowminded, militaristic state.

MARTINSON: (*Quietly*) What?

ELAINE: And as a matter of fact, I think it not funny at all. I think it a tragedy.

(*There is a pause. Then* MARTINSON *turns to appeal to the others.*)

STEPHEN *quiet, near* ANGELIS.)

STEPHEN: Has there been trouble?

ANGELIS: No. No trouble.

STEPHEN: I thought perhaps . . .

ANGELIS: What?

(*The furniture in the room is changed round by the* CREW, *setting it right.*)

STEPHEN: We had heard that Mehta was coming.

ANGELIS: Mehta is coming, yes.

(*He moves away, passing* ELAINE *who has collected her script.*) Monica, all well?

ELAINE: Fine, thank you.

(ANGELIS *turns, looking at the set.*)

ANGELIS: Please, now, everyone, we rehearse. It is what? It is the evening. The scene is evening. Peggy at last begins to have her doubts.

(STEPHEN *is waiting, refusing to give up.*)

STEPHEN: Have you spoken to Mehta?

ANGELIS: Only on the phone.

STEPHEN: And?

ANGELIS: It is true there are things he does not like in our production.

STEPHEN: Such as?

ANGELIS: I don't know.

STEPHEN: Angelis. Everyone here has heard rumours that the film is in danger.

(*A* PROPMAN *has appeared with an inappropriate pink-feathered fan.*)

PROPMAN: Where do I put this?

(*There is a sudden quiet. The* ELAINE *actress speaks with authority.*)

ELAINE: Speak for the company, Mike.

(*There is a moment before* ANGELIS *realizes he must square with the actors. Then:*)

ANGELIS: It is not him. It is Peggy.

STEPHEN: Peggy?

ANGELIS: Peggy came. She visited the set, you remember? Earlier today. She saw the action. It reminds her of the

MARTINSON: Did you hear what she just said?

M'BENGUE: (*Neutrally*) Yes, I did.

MARTINSON: (*Turning back to* ELAINE) Do you know what Sartre said?

ELAINE: Yes, I do.

(*There is a pause.*)
What *did* he say?

MARTINSON: Why say you did?

ELAINE: Well, I mean, I know what Sartre said about various things . . .

MARTINSON: Such as?

ELAINE: Well, I mean, I can't remember what things he said what about . . . I mean . . . I know he liked actresses very much . . .

(MARTINSON *ignores this.*)

MARTINSON: I will tell you what he said about Israel. That it was a historical exception.

(PEGGY *reappears, in a yellow dressing-gown this time.*)

PEGGY: This one?

MARTINSON: Very nice.

ELAINE: Sure.

(PEGGY *goes out again.*)

MARTINSON: That normally the Jews would have no right to the territory of Palestine, but that the crime against them was so great, that it was so out of proportion with anything any people had ever suffered before, that it was necessary to make a historical exception and say, 'Yes, give them the land.'

(*A pause.* ELAINE *concedes with ill grace.*)

ELAINE: OK.

MARTINSON: That's what Sartre said.

ELAINE: OK.

(M'BENGUE *has lent over casually and is looking down at* MARTINSON'*s discarded* Times.)

M'BENGUE: It's not Z anyway.

MARTINSON: What?

M'BENGUE: Look, six down is 'evasion'. You don't spell that with a Z. You spell it with an S.

MARTINSON: Are you telling me how to do this?

M'BENGUE: Which means fourteen across is now a seven-letter word beginning with S.

(MARTINSON *looks at him unkindly*.)

MARTINSON: I suppose you agree with *her*.

M'BENGUE: What?

MARTINSON: About the Jews.

(ELAINE *gets up from her chair, suddenly losing her temper*.)

ELAINE: For Christ's sake, man . . .

(PEGGY *has reappeared in stripes*.)

PEGGY: What do you think?

ELAINE: (*Shouts*) It sucks.

(*She throws up her hands in the air, apologizing*.)

I'm sorry. No, it's just . . . What are we doing? Where is Angelis?

PEGGY: I want to do the scene.

(*Everyone momentarily lost, before* STEPHEN *looks up again, mild, oblivious*.)

STEPHEN: Why are policemen so important in homosexual mythology?

M'BENGUE: Pardon?

STEPHEN: It's . . . I'm reading about E. M. Forster. What everyone admires in him is not . . . you know . . . *books*, I mean that's what he wrote, but what everyone really admires him for was having a boyfriend who was a policeman.

M'BENGUE: Well, it is an achievement.

STEPHEN: I suppose.

(*He smiles to himself*.)

P.C. Bob Buckingham.

(MARTINSON *is frowning, ready to hold forth again*.)

MARTINSON: But in a sense it's absolutely symbolic in a way, isn't it?

ELAINE: (*Quietly*) Oh, God.

MARTINSON: Surely what he was doing was forcing the authoritarian figure, in a sense, to yield . . . I'm just talking out loud here . . .

(ELAINE *looks across at* PEGGY, *close to murder. Then goes and lies down on the bed in the fake room*.)

54

In some way the father-figure, perhaps . . .

ELAINE: Oh, Jesus, where is Angelis?

MARTINSON: He was seducing him and in some way he was forcing him to admit that his authority was an act, that underneath the social role we all play, we are all . . .

STEPHEN: What?

MARTINSON: Well, you know . . .

STEPHEN: What?

(MARTINSON *pauses*.)

MARTINSON: Gay.

(STEPHEN *frowns, mystified*. MARTINSON *hastens to qualify*.)

I mean, not exclusively. We're not, exclusively. Obviously, you would know more about this. If you've seen those films about fish, it's clear. It's been proved biologically. Sometimes it's one thing, sometimes the other . . .

ELAINE: (*Calling from the bed*) And sometimes fuck-all if they're anything like the rest of us.

(MARTINSON *explodes*.)

MARTINSON: Will somebody please tell this woman . . .

STEPHEN: It's all right, honestly. She's just provoking you.

(STEPHEN *smiles, placating*. MARTINSON *goes on, the air tense*.)

MARTINSON: We pay a price for suppressing this truth. That we are all bisexual. We hide this fact at enormous expense to ourselves in order to obey some imaginary social norm. But the result of this suppression is great damage inside. Finally . . . yes . . . we implode.

STEPHEN: Yes, well . . .

MARTINSON: Literally!

STEPHEN: (*Puzzled*) It's a problem.

MARTINSON: Yes.

(*At once* ANGELIS *sweeps on, followed by* ASSISTANTS.)

ANGELIS: I am sorry, my friends . . .

PEGGY: Angelis!

ANGELIS: . . . I have been delayed. Crew!

(*All the actors get up as he calls out*.)

ELAINE: Thank God. We were all about to implode.

ANGELIS: Please, we move on, we prepare the scene.

(PEGGY *moves on to the set as* ELAINE *and* MARTINSON *leave it*.

55

original events—the event, the book, the film. Suddenly she panics. She is now—what?—an older woman, and she sees we are to re-enact a night of which she is no longer proud. Suddenly thinking . . . she realizes she was callous. Her actions seem cruel.

STEPHEN: Right.

ANGELIS: She goes back to Victor Mehta. She tries to stop the film.

STEPHEN: What?

ANGELIS: No, it is fine . . .

(ANGELIS *wanders over to the set.*)

ELAINE: The film is being stopped?

ANGELIS: There is a contractual argument, that is all, as to whether Victor Mehta has the right to approve the screenplay.

STEPHEN: Does he?

ANGELIS: In theory, perhaps. It is in his contract, yes, but the lawyers . . . you can imagine.

STEPHEN: Angelis—

ANGELIS: His solicitors have notified us of their intention to serve an injunction, and we have notified them of our intention to counterfile.

(*He stops, firm.*)

It is a game.

(*Then smiles, resuming his usual manner.*)

So meanwhile, until the resolution, we schedule rehearsal. Yes? Say nothing please.

STEPHEN: All right.

(*He walks away, unhappily.*)

ANGELIS: Please, we rehearse. I beg you, let us act.

(*A* PROPMAN *has appeared through the 'door' of the 'room' with an enormous bunch of flowers.*)

PROPMAN: You have flowers?

PEGGY: (*Delighted*) For me?

ANGELIS: No, no flowers. The flowers are downstairs.

(*The* MEHTA *actor has walked on and has sat down at the desk in the bedroom, taking his jacket off and putting it over the back of the chair.* PEGGY *has for some time been stretched out*

57

on top of the bed in her latest dressing-gown. They are silent, ready to go.)

Madeleine in her place. And Shashi, please . . . to work.

(The room is peaceful, ready for action, but the M'BENGUE actor is still standing in the middle.)

Er, John . . .

(M'BENGUE *turns and looks out.*)

M'BENGUE: 'Slavery'.

ANGELIS: What?

M'BENGUE: 'Slavery' is the word.

(There's a pause. Then he turns and walks silently out of the room.)

ANGELIS: OK.

(PEGGY, who is staring at the counterpane, now looks up, and Scene Six begins.)

PEGGY: How do you write a book?

MEHTA: *(Without looking up)* Mmm?

PEGGY: I mean, when you start out, do you know what you think?

MEHTA: No.

PEGGY: I don't mean the plot. I'm sure the plot's easy . . .

MEHTA: No, the plot's very hard.

PEGGY: Well, all right, the plot's hard. But what you *think* . . . do you know what you think?

MEHTA: No.

(He turns from writing in his notebook and looks at her.)

The act of writing is the act of discovering what you believe.

(He turns back to his work, smiling slightly.)

How do you act?

PEGGY: *(Smiles at once)* Oh, lord . . .

MEHTA: Well?

PEGGY: I mean, I don't. Not really. I'm not an actress. I'm too conscious. I'm too self-aware. I stand aside.

MEHTA: Does that mean you plan to give it up?

(PEGGY does not answer. She has already picked up a booklet which is beside her on the bed.)

58

PEGGY: Don't you love this country?

MEHTA: Why?

PEGGY: An airline timetable, I was looking . . .

MEHTA: Were you thinking of leaving?

PEGGY: No, listen, what I love about India, the only country in the world where they'd print poetry—here, look, at the bottom of the Kuwait–Delhi airline schedule. A poem. 'Some come to India to find themselves, some come to lose themselves . . .' In an *airline schedule*? Isn't that a pretty frightening admission?

(*He is about to speak seriously but she interrupts.*)

MEHTA: Peggy . . .

PEGGY: No, I wasn't leaving. How could I be leaving? I'm here to make a film.

MEHTA: But?

(*A pause. Then she looks away.*)

PEGGY: But at lunchtime I did something so stupid that the thought of going down those steps . . .

MEHTA: I see.

PEGGY: . . . into that lobby, along that corridor, past those delegates, into that deserted conference hall, for this appalling contest . . .

MEHTA: Yes.

PEGGY: . . . when all I want is to spend my time with you.

(*A pause.* MEHTA *sets aside his notebook.*)

MEHTA: American women, they make me laugh. I am at home.

PEGGY: Well, good.

MEHTA: It is like they pick you up in their lovemaking from wherever they last left off. At once, bang! and they're away. No matter with whom it was last time, if it was someone else, no matter, nevertheless, it is go at once. The passion again. Making love to an American woman, it is like climbing aboard an already moving train.

(PEGGY *smiles and gets off the bed to go to the bathroom.*)

PEGGY: We have needs.

MEHTA: I am sure.

PEGGY: (*Calling as she goes out*) We have no guilt. Americans are unashamed about their needs.

MEHTA: (*Smiles*) Yes.

PEGGY: (*Off*) When an Englishman has an emotion, his first instinct is to repress it. When an American has an emotion, his first instinct . . .

MEHTA: Ah well, yes . . .

PEGGY: (*Off*) They express it!

MEHTA: Usually at length.

PEGGY: (*Off*) Why not?

(MEHTA *sits smiling, contented, happy with* PEGGY *and able to show it clearly now she is out of the room.*)

MEHTA: Always examining their own reactions . . .

PEGGY: (*Off*) Yes.

MEHTA: Always analysing, always telling you what they feel—*I* think, *I* feel, let me tell you what *I* feel . . .

PEGGY: Sure.

MEHTA: The endless drama of it all.

(PEGGY *reappears at the bathroom door. She has taken off her dressing-gown and has changed into another loose cotton suit.*)

PEGGY: And which is better, tell me, Victor, next to the English? Which is healthier, eh?

(*He looks at her with great affection.*)

MEHTA: You make love like a wounded panther. You are like a paintshop on fire.

(*She looks at him. Then raises her eyebrows.*)

PEGGY: Well, goodness.

MEHTA: Yes.

PEGGY: Writer, eh?

(*He smiles. There is a knock at the door.* PEGGY *goes to answer it.*)

MEHTA: It comes in handy.

PEGGY: Is that what you say to all the girls? 'Thank you, that was wounded-panther-like.'

(*She opens the door. A* WAITER *is standing outside.*)

Yes?

WAITER: Mr Andrews. He is waiting downstairs.

(PEGGY *looks at the* WAITER *a moment, then nods.*)

PEGGY: Thank you.

(*She closes the door, stands a moment, her face turned away*

from MEHTA. *Then she turns, walks across to the dressing-table and picks up her hairbrush. Then, casually:*)
What about you?

MEHTA: What?

PEGGY: When are you thinking of leaving?

MEHTA: Oh . . . tomorrow.

PEGGY: Really?

MEHTA: Yes.
(*There is a pause. Then deliberately:*)
After I make my speech, I would hope.
(*There is a slight pause, then both of them speak at once.*)
Peggy . . .

PEGGY: I don't know. I can't say which of the two of you makes more sense to me. I've never had to choose, you see. Like so many people, I've never made a choice.
(*She turns and smiles at him.*)
Sitting at nights with my professors, sure, it was great. Philosophy, that was my major . . . eight arguments as to whether God exists.

MEHTA: Does he?

PEGGY: We never decided.

MEHTA: There you are.

PEGGY: But the game was fun. No question. Great nights. What are those things called? 'Angel Bars' we ate. Gloppy cherries covered in chocolate in a candy bar. To me there isn't a philosophical idea that isn't to do with food. Toasted marshmallows, late at night, when I first read Wittgenstein. I can still remember the taste of 'The world is all that is the case.' It tasted good, it still tastes good, that moment of understanding something. But *applying* it? Well, that's different, the world not offering so many opportunities for that sort of thing. Arts and humanities! Philosophy! What's the point in America, where the only philosophy you'll ever encounter is the philosophy of making money. In my case by taking off T-shirts. In fact, not even taking them off—I'm too up-market for that. I have only to hint there are situations in which I *would* show my breasts to certain people, certain *rich* people, that they do indeed exist under

61

there, but for now it's enough to suggest their shape, hint at
their shape, in a T-shirt. Often it will have to be wet. By
soaking my T-shirts in water I make my living. It's true.
Little to do with the life of ideas.

(*She smiles.*)

Spoilt. Spoilt doesn't say it, though that's what people say
about Americans, and spoilt, I suppose, is what I was till
lunchtime, till I made this ridiculous offer. A young idiot's
suicidal offer with which she is now going to have to learn
to live.

(*She turns and looks at* MEHTA.)

Well, good luck to you. Debate well, Victor, for on your
performance depends . . .

MEHTA: (*Smiles*) Don't tell me.

PEGGY: . . . my future. Tonight.

(*They stand a moment at opposite sides of the room, looking at
one another.*)

MEHTA: It's your fault.

PEGGY: Oh yes.

MEHTA: You with your 'Oh, Stephen is not such a bad fellow.'
He *is* a bad fellow. This you must learn.

(*The* WAITER *knocks on the door.* PEGGY *does not move, just
calls out, looking at* VICTOR *all the time.*)

PEGGY: Yes!

WAITER: Madam, Mr Andrews is asking why you are not
downstairs.

PEGGY: Tell him . . . tell him we are coming. Just one minute.
Mr Mehta is preparing his case.

(MEHTA *smiles at her, the two of them still not moving as the*
WAITER *is heard to go.*)

MEHTA: Give me a kiss.

PEGGY: No kisses. I am no longer yours. I belong now to the
winner of an argument.

(MEHTA *takes his jacket from the back of the chair, as she waits.
He puts it on. He puts his notebook in his pocket and turns to
her.*)

MEHTA: Fine.

(*Then he turns to the unseen* ANGELIS.)

Is that all right?

ANGELIS: (*Off*) Yes. Smile at the end.

(ANGELIS *walks thoughtfully on to the set, and we are into* Scene Seven.)

OK, let's go on. Madeleine?

PEGGY: Yes.

(*He turns and sees that the* PEGGY *actress has not moved but is standing still, as if about to cry.*)

ANGELIS: Are you all right?

PEGGY: Oh, I'm sorry. I . . .

(ANGELIS *holds up a tactful hand at an approaching* CREWMAN.)

ANGELIS: Hold it.

PEGGY: No.

MEHTA: OK, sweetheart.

PEGGY: Yes . . . no . . . I'm sorry, it's silly. No, I just . . . I was doing the scene, I'd never really thought about it.

(*She is suddenly assertive.*)

How awful for her. That she unthinkingly . . . I mean, her innocence.

(*She looks at them. Then, anticlimactically, she begins to apologize again.*)

I don't know, I guess I'd never really thought.

ANGELIS: (*Relieved*) OK, right, take the flat out.

CREWMAN: OK, guv.

(*The wall is slowly flown, the bed removed, the furniture quietly taken out. Behind lies the conference area. The* STEPHEN *actor is at the very back, going through his lines with the* SCRIPT GIRL. *The* MAKE-UP GIRL *waits with* PEGGY's *shoes.*)

MEHTA: You don't think, I know. It's the same with me. 'He's so *nice* here.'

PEGGY: (*Laughs*) Yes.

MEHTA: When he's with Peggy, he's charming. Then when he goes downstairs to the debate, it's like he's not the same person at all. It's a double standard. It's only as you do it that the truth of it comes home.

(*The* ELAINE *actress wanders on with a cup of coffee and takes a seat on the now enormous area.* ANGELIS *turns to* PEGGY, *who has put on the shoes. He is still worried but does not want to show it.*)

You are all right, though?

PEGGY: Of course.

ANGELIS: It's just . . .

PEGGY: You want me to go on?

ANGELIS: If you don't mind.

PEGGY: No, of course. It was only just . . . realizing.

(*She goes and sits near* ELAINE *and smiles at her.* MEHTA *sits down too.*)

ELAINE: OK, darling?

(ANGELIS *stands and surveys the whole scene. It is very formal. The atmosphere after* PEGGY's *outburst is very quiet and tense. He nods at* STEPHEN.)

ANGELIS: Michael. Go on.

(*There is a pause. Then* STEPHEN, *with the* SCRIPT GIRL *beside him, starts quietly.*)

STEPHEN: 'The thirst for ideals is at the very heart of things. We may say a people needs ideals as they need bread. As great as the need for bread is the need for ideals.'

(STEPHEN *walks up to where the other actors are. The* SCRIPT GIRL *goes out, like a trainer leaving her athlete.*)

'The writer serves that need. He should be happy to serve it.'

(*He sits down opposite* MEHTA *in formal debating position, and at once, as if on cue,* MEHTA *gets up.*

Scene Eight *begins.*)

MEHTA: What nonsense! I cannot listen to this man.

PEGGY: Victor, you have agreed.

MEHTA: I know, I know.

PEGGY: For me.

MEHTA: I know what I have done . . .

(*He stands glowering across the room at* STEPHEN.)

I have tied myself to a night of stupidity.

(*He turns and walks away.*)

At lunchtime when you came to propose this confrontation, yes, I said, fine, because I knew I would win. As I shall win. Because my case is unarguably correct. But I had not reckoned . . .

PEGGY: Victor!

MEHTA: . . . on the sheer indignity. Even to have to *listen* to such
peasant-like ideas.

(STEPHEN *just smiles, calm, not rising to the bait.*)

STEPHEN: You speak all the time as if everything were decided.
As if you, Victor Mehta, are a finished human being, and
beneath you lies the world with all its intolerable
imperfections. As if you were objective and had no part in
its emotions. Yet some of its worst emotions you exhibit
very clearly.

MEHTA: Such as?

STEPHEN: Jealousy.

MEHTA: What do you mean?

STEPHEN: If I mention a novelist, if I mention Graham Greene...

MEHTA: A charlatan. Beneath contempt.

STEPHEN: Ah, well, you see. Exactly.

MEHTA: What?

STEPHEN: Your views on other writers.

MEHTA: No! An objective fact! A buffoon! A fool!

STEPHEN: You see! A ribbon of abuse. Pavlovian. At the very
mention of the name.

(MEHTA *looks at him mistrustfully, caught out a little.*)

MEHTA: So?

STEPHEN: So in matters which truly concern you, you are far
from objective. On the contrary, when things come too near
to you, then you fight from your own corner . . .

MEHTA: Like everyone.

STEPHEN: You fight those things that truly threaten you. In the
way Greene threatens you because he is a good writer.

MEHTA: Balls!

STEPHEN: In the way you will fight tomorrow for the right to
make fiction. And why? Why do writers insist on their right
to distort reality? You demand it in order to make better *|*
jokes.

(MEHTA *looks back at him. Then takes him on, beginning
quietly.*)

MEHTA: I was born in Bihar, of good family, my father a

schoolteacher who died in middle age. My mother died
when I was born. A brick-red, hot village on a plain. Baking
in the sun. That was my life for fourteen years, seeking
tuition where I could, seeking by the formulation of
sentences not to escape from the reality into which I was
born, but to set it in order. The setting of things in order,
that has always been my aim.

(STEPHEN *looks across to* PEGGY, *but she is listening intently.*)
It never occurred to me from that village that I should not
one day seek civilization. The heroes of the world are its
engineers, its doctors, its legislators—yes, there are things in
the old Empire I admired, that I was bound to admire,
because it is clear to any man born into boastful chaos that
order is desirable, and the agents of that order must be
practical men. I went to London, to the university there, to
the country where once medicine, education, the law had
been practised *sans pareil*, and found instead a country now
full of sloth and complacency—oh yes, on that we'd agree—
a deceitful, inward-looking ruling class blundering by its
racialism and stupidity into Suez. This was bitter for a boy
from an Indian village.

(*He shrugs slightly.*)
It seems when people become prosperous, they lose the urge
to improve themselves. Anyone who comes new to a society,
as I did, an immigrant, has his priorities clear: to succeed in
that society, to seek practical achievement, to educate his
children to the highest level. Yet somehow once one or two
generations have established their success, their
grandchildren rush the other way, to disown that success, to
disown its responsibilities, to seek by dressing as savages and
eating brown rice to discredit the very civilization their
grandfathers worked so hard to create. This seems to me the
ultimate cruelty . . .

PEGGY: Yes . . .

MEHTA: . . . the ultimate charade: that the young in the West
should dare to turn their faces at this time to the Third
World and cast doubt on the value of their own material
prosperity. Not content with flaunting its wealth, the West

66

now fashionably pretends that the materialism that has produced this wealth is not a good thing. Well, at least give us a chance to find out, say the poor. For God's sake let us practise this contempt ourselves. Instead of sending the Third World doctors and mechanics, we now send them hippies, and Marxist thinkers, and animal conservationists, and ecologists, and wandering fake Zen Buddhist students, who hasten to reassure the illiterate that theirs is a superior life to that of the West. What hypocrisy! The confrontation of the decadent with the primitive, the faithless with the barbarian. Reason overthrown, as it is now overthrown all over the world! For where, I ask you, was it that a man was meant to look for reason? Where was it that the world agreed it should be consecrated? Here. Yes, here. At meetings such as this. Assembled by the vast civil service of this now-futile United Nations—

STEPHEN: Futile? Why futile?

MEHTA: Futile because it does no good.

(*He gets up again, shouting.*)

Words! Meaningless words! Reports! So many reports that they boast from New York alone there flow annually United Nations documents which, laid end to end at the Equator, would stretch four times round the world! Yes! Half a billion pages! And this . . . this week one of the year's seven thousand major UN meetings. With working papers, proposals, counter-proposals, records, summaries. A bureaucracy drowning in its own words and suffocating in its own documents. The wastepaper basket the only instrument of sanity in an otherwise insane organization. Last year a Special Committee on the Rationalization and Organization of the General Assembly was set up to examine the problems of excessive documentation. It produced a report. *It was two hundred and nineteen pages long.* I ask you, what fiction can there be to compare with this absurdity? What writer could dream up this impossible decadence?

(*He stands shaking his head.*)

No, I tell you there is only one thing I know, and one only:

67

that in this universe of idiocy, the only thing we may rely on is the lone voice—the lone voice of the writer—who speaks only when he has something to say.

STEPHEN: Nonsense!

MEHTA: A voice that is pledged to individual integrity.

STEPHEN: My God! What a delusion!

ELAINE: It is a bit rich.

MEHTA: *Why?*

(*He turns.*)

(*Firmly*) Mankind has one enemy only and it is not poverty. It is self-deception. Yes . . .

(*He holds a hand up, anticipating* STEPHEN's *objection.*)

That finally is my case against you, Stephen. If Miss le Fanu is to adjudicate . . .

ELAINE: I am.

MEHTA: Then please remember that my case stands or falls here: that often from the best intentions we tell ourselves lies. Here—my God!—a conference run by the United Nations is a monument built to commemorate self-deception on the grandest scale. We would like it to work and so we pretend it does. And yet in our hearts—when we are not on our feet, Stephen, and making speeches, not in rooms where words fly up—in our hearts we know the UN is a palace of lies, run by a bureaucracy whose only interest is in the maintenance of its own prosperity. Forty per cent of UNESCO's income is spent in the administration of its own Paris office. A fact. A fact which I have mentioned in my books and for which I am attacked. I am told to point it out is bloody-minded and—what?—'unhelpful'. And yet to me, I am telling you, not to point it out is worse.

(*He stands a moment, nodding.*)

Tomorrow I must speak because not to speak is not to be a writer, not to be a man.

(*Then he looks away to* STEPHEN, *opening his hands as if to say, 'That's it.'*)

That, there, is where I yield. I have had the floor.

STEPHEN: Indeed.

(STEPHEN *looks at* MEHTA *a moment. Then when he replies it is*

68

with a new and unsuspected warmth.)

We've pretended, you and I, that the debate between us is not to do with personality, only with issues . . .

MEHTA: That's so.

STEPHEN: But in fact, if I've learnt anything in the last twenty-four hours, it is that no argument is pure, it's always a compound. Partly the situation, partly temper, partly whim . . . sometimes just pulled out of the air and often from the worst motives. Peggy, no offence . . .

PEGGY: I understand.

(*She smiles.*)

STEPHEN: I've grown up here. In this hotel. I came like a boy, a 27-year-old boy, and I can't help feeling whichever way the contest falls, I'm going to leave a man, partly because I've grown fond of you, Victor.

MEHTA: (*Deadpan*) Really?

STEPHEN: And I think I've felt . . . some growing generosity from you, too, especially this evening. You've stopped calling me Andrews. You call me Stephen, perhaps because even if you don't agree with me, you nevertheless now recognize me. Perhaps even as an element in yourself.

MEHTA: A sentimental line of argument.

STEPHEN: Yes. If I am to win, I must attack the man.

(PEGGY *looks across to* MEHTA, *slightly alarmed. But* MEHTA *does not react.*)

I am arguing that tomorrow you must go out and denounce your own fiction, because it will be your last remaining chance to rejoin the human race.

(*A burst of reaction, even* MEHTA *surprised.*)

MEHTA: Well!

PEGGY: My God.

ELAINE: Original.

STEPHEN: Everything you say, everything you propose, is from a position of superiority and hopelessness. 'What can one do?' you say, grabbing at one depressing piece of information after another, almost—I put it to you—as if you personally were a man now almost frightened of hope.

MEHTA: Absurd!

STEPHEN: Oh yes, the gleam that comes into your eye when you have some dismal statistic. 'Sixty-five per cent of people who set out to cross roads get run over,' you say with a satisfied beam, as if their presumption had been justly rewarded. Whereas you, of course . . . The position of the habitual non-road-crosser has been wholly vindicated!
(*He gestures into the air.*)
From way up there you claim to see things clearly. 'The truth,' you say, 'the lone voice.' But in fact your so-called truthfulness is nothing but the projection of your own isolation, and of your own despair. Because you do a job which is lonely and hard, because *you* spend all day locked in a room, so you project your loneliness on to the world.

MEHTA: No.

STEPHEN: Partly from anger at your own way of life, you try to discredit the work of other people—out there—a lot of whom have pleasanter jobs than you.
(*He pauses. Then, with a smile.*),
Jealousy . . .

MEHTA: No.

STEPHEN: There is jealousy there. The jealousy of a man who does not take part, who no longer knows how to take part, but can only *write*.
(PEGGY *looks across to* MEHTA, *who has turned away.*)
Oh yes. And the more you write, the more isolated you become. The more frozen.
(*There is a pause.*)

MEHTA: No.

STEPHEN: (*Smiles*) You come here to this conference not to publicize your work, or to express your position—what would be the point? Your position is so complete, so *closed*, there is little point in expounding it. No, you come to scrape around—yes, like the rest of us, to scrape around for contact . . .
(*A pause. Then* PEGGY *suddenly seems embarrassed, confused.*)

PEGGY: No, please, it's . . .

STEPHEN: What?

PEGGY: Unfair.

70

STEPHEN: Why?

PEGGY: Victor is . . . too nice a man for this.

(STEPHEN *turns back*, MEHTA *himself still impassive.*)

STEPHEN: Your wife, your child, you leave behind in England . . .

(*He looks quickly to* PEGGY, *who plainly knows nothing of wife or child.*)

Oh yes. Come here. Five thousand miles. Make love to Peggy Whitton. Leave. The last emotions left. Jealousy, yes. And lust. What is left in you that is not disdainful, that is not dead? Only jealousy and lust.

(*There is a silence.* ELAINE *looks between them, warning.*)

ELAINE: Stephen . . .

(*But* STEPHEN *is leaning forward to make his main point.*)

STEPHEN: You will never understand any struggle unless you take part in it. How easy to condemn this organization as absurd. Of course. I've sat here and sweated and bitched and argued . . . often with Elaine . . .

ELAINE: It's true.

STEPHEN: I've run screaming from the points of order and the endless 'I am mandated to ask . . .' But why do you not think that at the centre of the verbiage, often only by hazard but nevertheless at times and unpredictably, crises *are* averted, aid *is* directed?

MEHTA: I dare say.

STEPHEN: Why do you not imagine that if you stopped distancing yourself, if you got rid of your wretched fastidiousness, you could not lend yourself for once not to *objection* but to getting something done?

(STEPHEN *sits back, contemptuous.*)

Oh, no, it's too hard. Never—the risk of failure too great. Like so many clever men, you move steadily to the right, further, further, distancing, always distancing yourself, building yourself a bunker into which only the odd woman is occasionally allowed, disowning your former ideals . . .

MEHTA: You know nothing.

STEPHEN: . . . attacking those who still have those ideals with a ferocity which is way out of proportion to their crime.

(MEHTA *suddenly stirred.*)

MEHTA: No!

STEPHEN: Yes! Well, move, move to the right if you wish to. Join
the shabby crew if you want to. Go in the way people do.
But at least spare us the books, spares us the Stations of the
Cross, the public announcements. Make your move in
private, do it in private, like a sexual pervert, do it privately.
Move with a mac over your knee to the right, but spare *us*,
spare your audience, spare those who have to watch one
good man after another go down.

PEGGY: Stephen, it is too much.

ELAINE: Please.

STEPHEN: No!

(*He has stood up.*)

The revenge of the old! All the time! The history of the
world is the revenge of the old, as they paint themselves
into corners, loveless, removed, relieved occasionally in hotel
rooms by the visits of strange women, who come to tell them
that, yes, they are doing well and, yes, they may now take
revenge on those who are still young. People, countries, the
same thing; the world now full of young countries who are
trying imperfect, unwieldy new systems of ordering their
affairs, watched by the old who are praying that they will
not succeed . . .

(*He shakes his head. Then suddenly:*)

If you wish to rejoin us, if you wish to be human, go out
tomorrow and parrot whatever rubbish you are handed and
at least experience an emotion which is not disdain.

MEHTA: I would not give you the pleasure.

STEPHEN: I shall not be here.

MEHTA: What?

STEPHEN: A midnight train leaves for Ahmadabad and on to
Jaipur. Frankly . . .

(*He smiles and crosses the room.*)

. . . my time is being wasted here.

ELAINE: Stephen . . .

(STEPHEN *has collected his abandoned briefcase.*)

PEGGY: What are you doing?

(STEPHEN *has turned to* PEGGY.)

STEPHEN: Peggy, I'm sorry. Your offer, it was kind, more than tempting. But all afternoon, all evening, I realized . . . also absurd. My own fault. For years I've apologized. A shambler, a neurotic, almost by definition, I've accepted the picture the world has of an idealist as a man who is necessarily a clown. No shortage of people to tell him he's a fool. And we accept this picture. Yes, we betray our instincts. We betray them because we're embarrassed, and we've lost our conviction that we can make what's best in us prevail.
(*He smiles, and he is now ready to go.*)
Well, enough—I'm sorry—

PEGGY: (*Smiles*) Stephen . . .

STEPHEN: . . . of all that.
(*He takes her hand a moment.*)
Here, somehow, these strange events . . . falling, like Alice, into this argument . . . meeting this man, the act of suddenly deciding what I feel . . . No more apology. Hold to my beliefs.
(*He turns to* ELAINE.)
Elaine, I owe you lunch.

ELAINE: (*Getting up to embrace him*) Stephen . . .

STEPHEN: Thank you. Send my best to America. I withdraw from the contest. What you must do only you can decide.
(*He turns and goes out. The three of them left behind. There is silence.*)
(MEHTA *looks down. Then darkly:*)

MEHTA: I should not have come here. I am going upstairs.
(*He goes out. The two women are left alone on the stage.* PEGGY *looks down.*)

PEGGY: It's my fault. Now I'm going to get drunk.
(*And as she looks up, the lights fade to darkness, as much like a film fade as possible. There is a pause in the dark. Then the sound of banging at the back. From far away* MEHTA's *voice, a stick beating at a door, and* Scene Nine *has begun.*)

MEHTA: Hello. Please. Is there anyone?
(*At once, in the darkness, the sound of an* ASSISTANT *scurrying across the set.*)

ASSISTANT: Coming! Coming!

(At the very back of the stage, far further than we realized the stage reached, a door opens, and brilliant light pours through it. Silhouetted in the doorway stands MEHTA.*)*

My God!

MEHTA: I am Victor Mehta.

ASSISTANT: Ah, yes. You were expected earlier.

(He turns, panicking slightly.)

Everyone! Please! Is there a light there?

(He turns to MEHTA.*)*

Please wait.

MEHTA: I am waiting.

(A single light comes on in the grid and we see the stage is now black. An empty film studio. ANGELIS *is rushing on, in the last stages of pulling his trousers up.)*

ANGELIS: Ah, my goodness, you are here. We were expecting you earlier.

*(*MEHTA *has come right down. He is now a more formidable man, in a camelhair coat, heavier, less dapper.* ANGELIS *shakes his hand.)*

An honour.

MEHTA: You are pulling on your trousers.

ANGELIS: A friend.

(He elaborates needlessly, embarrassed.)

In make-up.

MEHTA: I see.

ANGELIS: A drink?

(An ASSISTANT *has brought a chair, but* MEHTA *has wandered away.)*

MEHTA: Mr Angelis, I cannot pretend I am glad to come here.

ANGELIS: You have read the script?

MEHTA: I cannot read five pages.

ANGELIS: *(To his* ASSISTANT*)* Thank you.

(The ASSISTANT *goes.)*

No, well, admittedly . . . there *are* weaknesses—

MEHTA: The dialogue. When they open their mouths, dead frogs fall out.

ANGELIS: Yes, well, certainly . . . it can do with polishing . . .

74

MEHTA: A moral story has been reduced to the status of a
romance, transferred to a vulgar medium and traduced. Very
well. It is what one expects. One looks to the cinema for
money, not for enlightenment. And to be fair, the money
has arrived.

(*He turns and faces* ANGELIS.)

It is in the matter of meaning I have come.

ANGELIS: Meaning?

MEHTA: Meaning, Mr Angelis.

ANGELIS: Ah, yes.

(MEHTA *looks at him. Then starts afresh.*)

MEHTA: The film is being made for one reason. On my name, is
that right?

ANGELIS: Well, not exactly.

MEHTA: Because I am famous, my name raises money. A subject
which would normally be considered too literary, too talky,
becomes a feature film.

ANGELIS: In part.

MEHTA: And yet what is literary, what is at the heart of the
novel, this is exactly what your film destroys.

(*A pause.* MEHTA *sits.*)

ANGELIS: I see.

MEHTA: There is a balance in the book. Each of the characters is
forced to examine the values of his or her life.

ANGELIS: Yes.

MEHTA: The novelist is accused of dalliance and asked to put a
value on what he has seen as a passing affair. The actress
questions her easy promiscuity and is made to realize
adulthood will involve choice. And the journalist assumes
the confidence of his own beliefs.

ANGELIS: And is killed.

MEHTA: Killed, yes.

(*There is a pause.*)

You show this?

ANGELIS: Of course. We have a train.

(MEHTA *looks at him. Another pause.*)

MEHTA: In a sense, I care nothing. A book is written. It is left
behind you to be misinterpreted by a thousand critics. How

75

much to say, how much to leave out, these fine, judicious decisions over which writers agonize are soon rendered meaningless by the collision of what is written on the page and what is already there in the reader's mind. The reader brings to the book his own preconceptions, prejudices perhaps. He misreads sentences. Insignificant words that seem to you bland carry for him or her some huge significance. A tiny incident in the narrative is for one person the key to the book's interpretation; to another it is where he accidentally turns two pages and misses it altogether. So if you come . . . if you make a film, you reinterpret. Maybe it is only for our own private satisfaction we insist on one meaning and yet . . . in a way your film is a betrayal unless at the heart it is clear: for all the bitterness, for all the stupidity . . . you must see, we admired this young man.

(*A pause.* MEHTA *sits back.*)

Of course, death, death brings him dignity, but also in truth, even at the time . . .

(MEHTA *looks away.* ANGELIS *waits tactfully.*)

ANGELIS: Yes, well, that's clear.

MEHTA: Clear to you, perhaps. Yes, your intention. But is it there in the script? Peggy couldn't see it when she visited this morning. That, when she told me, was the heart of her complaint. She thought the script made Stephen foolish.

ANGELIS: I see. Is that all?

MEHTA: No. The death.

ANGELIS: Ah.

MEHTA: And the way you tell it.

ANGELIS: I see.

MEHTA: There is something there. An emotion I had.

(*There is a pause. Then, soberly*:)

Certainly we drove, as you suggest it. As soon as we heard, Peggy came to my room. We found a taxi-driver. All the way from Bombay he smoked marijuana. Thirty miles out Peggy and I demanded to change cabs. Another drive, the day beginning to get hot. And we knew, long before we reached the disaster, just how close the disaster was. Small

groups of people at first; driving further, more people. Now in larger groups, now more excited, finally crowds, in the middle of the valley. A valley like any other but for the crowds. We had expected a corpse. A body on its own, we had thought. It was impossible even to get close to the carriages which had overturned. All one side, people had clung to the framework and been crushed. A single cow had strayed on to the line. Forty more miles to the mortuary . . . to unidentified bodies . . . paperwork . . . hysteria . . . the heat. And the conference itself was suddenly rendered ridiculous. Whatever meaning it once had was now lost. As tomorrow . . . in this barn, the lights will burn, the camera will turn, a predetermined script will be acted out by men and women who know it has been robbed of sense.
(*He nods.*)
What can stop your chaps from rising from their beds tomorrow at 7.30? The machine turns of its own volition! Oh, the will that is needed to bring it to a halt!
(*He smiles, bitter.*)
I was not there, and M'Bengue denounced me. Yes! In savage terms. 'This fascist novelist, this charlatan, who, when the moment comes, ducks the chance to defend his indefensible work . . .'
(*A pause.*)
I was not there. I was at the accident.

ANGELIS: Of course.
(*A silence.* ANGELIS *uneasy.*)
But surely when people realized, I mean, your reason, *why* you weren't there . . .

MEHTA: Why should they care? The whole conference was longing for a dogfight. What a disappointment when it did not occur.
(*He shakes his head.*)
Even in death, appropriation. Especially in death, perhaps. Experience appropriated and vomited forth. Everything that suits us we place upon our map. As soon as the news reached them, Stephen's death was exploited in an encomium of lies. 'On a railway line outside Surat lies the

77

young body of a Third World ally . . .'

(*He turns away, the old* MEHTA.)

My God! What hypocrisy! Trash!

(ANGELIS *is puzzled. Gently:*)

ANGELIS: Yes, but surely those *were* his opinions. Why do you object? That's what he believed in. I mean, by your argument we would all say nothing.

MEHTA: Yes. I suppose.

(*He turns sadly and looks at* ANGELIS.)

The book was clear. I was moved by what happened, and later that day I made a choice. The conference could continue without me. This you do not mention, but you must make it clear. I chose to be silent. In memory of Stephen . . . I stayed away.

ANGELIS: I see. Yes. I'd not understood that. This morning when Peggy came, we thought the problem was more to do with character.

MEHTA: No.

ANGELIS: If what you're after is this feeling that everything is meaningless, then, of course, we will put that in as well. A slight dialogue adjustment, a page maybe. Then it is clear.

(*There is a pause. The* STEPHEN *actor has appeared at the back, dressed in baggy trousers and an expensive coat. Soft-spoken. The* PEGGY *actress is standing behind him, dressed very young in a smart coat and jeans.*)

STEPHEN: Oh, I'm sorry. Are we interrupting?

ANGELIS: Michael . . .

STEPHEN: We were half-way to Belgravia before I realized I'd forgotten . . .

(MEHTA *is staring at him.*)

MEHTA: You are he.

STEPHEN: . . . my script.

(*Then* STEPHEN *makes a formal move towards* MEHTA, *the* PEGGY *actress following a little nervously behind.*)

Mr Mehta?

(*He turns to introduce the* PEGGY *actress but* MEHTA, *overcome, has turned away, not taking his hand.*)

Madeleine . . .

MEHTA: I don't know. For some reason I am moved.

(*The other three stand, uncertain.* PEGGY *and* STEPHEN *look fresh and scrubbed and absurdly young.* STEPHEN *looks nervously at* ANGELIS.)

STEPHEN: Angelis here said you weren't happy with the text.

MEHTA: I cannot begin to say. Everything is wrong.

(*He turns back, recovering.* STEPHEN *at his most diffident and charming.*)

STEPHEN: I can see from the outside it must be discomforting. Film is. It's so fractured, so broken up. To look at, at first, the first impression is chaos. As with India, I imagine, to the Western visitor. Nothing makes sense on the surface. Then, by a process, one absorbs. One is patient. The tendons of the place begin to show through.

(MEHTA *looks at him with respect.* PEGGY, *emboldened, smiles.*)

PEGGY: We can't be doing what you want, Mr Mehta. We're aware of it, for ours is bound to be a love story. A commercial picture with, eventually, after the studio, some exotic locations. Sex and death are really the standout features, rather than the arguments in the book, some of which we *are* filming . . . all of which, I guess, we think, will be cut.

(*They smile, only* ANGELIS *uneasy.*)

STEPHEN: This, by any prevailing standard, is a picture of integrity. Can you imagine? Even though they've put in a scene where Elaine bathes topless in the holy river. It's hard to believe. Two thousand Indians in dhotis and she takes her top off. A reporter? From CBS?

(ANGELIS *looks silently resentful.*)

PEGGY: Quite apart from how the holy river . . .

MEHTA: It is not in Bombay.

STEPHEN: Quite. It's a thousand miles away. That small detail apart . . .

(ANGELIS *sulky on his own, as the others smile.*)

ANGELIS: It is not true. She is to bathe in the tank.

(STEPHEN *points to his own forehead.*)

STEPHEN: We have this book here, however.

MEHTA: Thank you.

STEPHEN: In our heads. This blunderer . . .

(*He gestures amiably at* ANGELIS.)

Me, an actor of limited ability. Madeleine, God bless her, who is reading Herodotus—can you imagine?—to get into the part.

(*The* PEGGY *actress blushes and looks at her feet.*)

'Reading Herodotus?' I said casually one day. 'Oh, you know,' she said, 'just skimming.'

(MEHTA *smiles, touched.*)

All the warmth, all the kindness we can bring, we will bring.

MEHTA: Thank you. That is something, I suppose.

(*He stands a moment, the whole group still. Then, resigned*:)

For the rest, of course, let it be toplessness . . .

STEPHEN: What else?

MEHTA: And bad dialogue. What else?

PEGGY: No sauna scene so far, but we're expecting one.

(MEHTA *nods slightly, the joke shared. Then* STEPHEN *makes to go.*)

STEPHEN: If you like, I can drive you back to London.

MEHTA: That will be good.

STEPHEN: I'll just get my things.

(*He goes out to the dressing-rooms.*)

PEGGY: Excuse me.

(PEGGY *follows him.*)

MEHTA: Mr Angelis, farewell. Thank you for listening.

ANGELIS: No.

(*He shakes* MEHTA's *hand.*)

If we can do it as you wish, we shall be pleased.

(*He goes out.* MEHTA *is left momentarily alone on the huge, empty stage. Then he turns his head and at once* MARTINSON *walks on, eerily quiet, and, from the other direction,* M'BENGUE. Scene Ten. *The lights change. A sinister calm.*)

MARTINSON: Monsieur M'Bengue . . .

(*The two men stand still opposite each other, formally, in the centre of the stage.*)

Your speech was excellent.

M'BENGUE: Yes. I admired this young man. So few whites have any understanding.

MARTINSON: The occasion was perfectly handled. And in a way, although tragic—the tragedy eats into my soul—but also, we must say, the way things fell out has also been elegant.

M'BENGUE: Elegant?

MARTINSON: Convenient.

(M'BENGUE *looks at him with silent contempt.*)

M'BENGUE: I see.

MARTINSON: Mr Mehta's necessary absence certainly removed the problems we had had.

(M'BENGUE *looks at him a moment, still quiet, still calm.*)

M'BENGUE: Mr Martinson, overnight I have been reading the conditions, the terms, of the aid you are proposing to give. They are stiff.

MARTINSON: They are exacting, yes. No aid is pure. There is always an element of trade in all such arrangements, and trade, after all, benefits both sides.

M'BENGUE: Surplus corn, surplus grain from America, at a commercial price . . .

MARTINSON: Less than the market price.

M'BENGUE: A considerable price.

(MARTINSON *smiles.*)

MARTINSON: Perhaps.

M'BENGUE: The other part of the package, the facility of a loan from the World Bank.

MARTINSON: That's right.

M'BENGUE: At 13 per cent. And not even that is the limit of it. With a demand for changes in the internal policies of our country . . .

MARTINSON: Adjustments, yes.

M'BENGUE: . . . deflation of the currency . . .

MARTINSON: Well . . .

M'BENGUE: . . . high internal interest rates.

MARTINSON: Strict monetary measures.

(*He smiles again.*)

Good housekeeping, yes.

M'BENGUE: A recognition that younger countries cannot expect to have social security systems. In sum, the destruction of the policies which brought our government into being. You

81

throw us a lifeline. The lifeline is in the shape of a noose.
(MARTINSON *shrugs slightly.*)

MARTINSON: Well, I think you will find it's not necessarily that
sinister. Certainly, over the five-year period the bank is
insisting, for its own protection, on certain parameters—is
that the word? There may well be some hardship at first. A
largely agricultural country like your own, peasant-based: one
would expect things to be hard when such measures are
introduced. Five years', ten years' belt-tightening. Suffering.
Comparative. Then, well, surely . . . you'll be out of the
woods.

(*He gestures to one side.*)

Shall we go through? There's a final dinner. We were going
to have pheasant, but it was generally felt, for a symbolic
gesture, it being the last night, each one of us will eat a
single bowl of rice. I hope it's all right.

(*He is about to go.*)

Oh, by the way, you will not refuse it?

M'BENGUE: The loan I cannot. I shan't eat the rice.

(M'BENGUE *turns and goes out.* MARTINSON, *left alone, turns
and goes out the other way.* MEHTA *stands alone, then the*
PEGGY *actress reappears at the other side of the stage. He
smiles absently at her. There is an embarrassed silence between
them,* MEHTA *still thinking about the scene which has just
passed.*)

MEHTA: Do you have children?

PEGGY: Oh no. No, I don't. You have a son?

MEHTA: By my first marriage, yes. I have custody. He lives with
Peggy and me. He's sixteen. A boy. He wants to change the
world.

PEGGY: Well, I guess . . . that's the best thing to do with it.

(*The actress smiles.*)

I'd like to meet him.

MEHTA: And he no doubt you.

(*He stands a moment.*)

This feeling, finally, that we may change things—this is at
the centre of everything we are. Lose that . . . lose that,
lose everything.

(*He stands, the man who has lost.*)

PEGGY: I'm sorry. I didn't catch what you said.

(*The* STEPHEN *actor returns, yet more cheerful than before.*)

STEPHEN: I have an open car. I hope that's all right. It can be a bit cold. It's a steel-grey, 2.4 litre 1954 Alvis. A Grey Lady. With real running boards. This thick. Not very practical for the English winter. But it is so beautiful.

(*He looks at* MEHTA.)

It's my whole life.

MEHTA: Yes. I am sure.

(*Distantly, music begins to play.* MEHTA *moves a few paces towards the door, then turns, suddenly cheered.*)

Madeleine. Michael. To London. Let's go.

(*He lifts his arms, the music swells and the lights go out.*)

BIRKBECK LIBRARY COLLEGE

828
HAR2
MAP

Birkbeck College

19 0028795 8